NIGHT TERRORS
STORIES OF SHADOW AND SUBSTANCE

NIGHT TERRORS

STORIES OF SHADOW AND SUBSTANCE

J
cop. 4

EDITED BY
LOIS DUNCAN

Simon & Schuster Books for Young Readers

SIMON & SCHUSTER BOOKS FOR YOUNG READERS
An imprint of Simon & Schuster Children's Publishing Division
1230 Avenue of the Americas, New York, New York 10020

Book design by Paul Zakris. The text for this book is set in 11-point Galliard
Printed and bound in the United States of America
First Edition
10 9 8 7 6 5 4 3 2 1

Library of Congress Cataloging-in-Publication Data

Night terrors : stories of shadow and substance / edited by Lois Duncan. — 1st ed.
         p.   cm.
Contents: The monkey's wedding / Joan Aiken — Satan's shadow / Alane Ferguson — The chosen / Madge Harrah — The bogey man / Annette Curtis Klause — Bearing Paul / Chris Lynch — The beautiful thing / Harry Mazer — The house on Buffalo Street / Norma Fox Mazer — The dark beast of death / Joan Lowery Nixon — Girl at the window / Richard Peck — The grind of an axe / Theodore Taylor — Moon kill / Patricia Windsor.
ISBN 0-689-80346-X
1. Horror tales, American. 2. Children's stories, American.
[1. Horror stories. 2. Short stories.] I. Duncan, Lois, 1934-
PZ5.N465 1996
[Fic]—dc20 95-44901

This collection of stories is dedicated to private investigator Pat Caristo, a light in the darkness.

CONTENTS

FOREWORD
BY LOIS DUNCAN

Throughout history, night has been considered a time of eeriness, mystery, and terror. And with good reason. When the sun goes down, the world as we know it disappears, and we are thrust into an alien environment filled with unseen dangers.

In the dark, inanimate objects become our enemies. The ropes of the friendly backyard swing become nooses, lashing out from the shadows to encircle our throats. Trees spring up like sentinels to block our passage across what we remember as unrestricted areas, and flowering bushes that delighted our senses in the daytime slash and stab at our faces with thorny fingers.

Night casts a spell upon animals, reminding them of their heritage and regressing them to prehistoric predators. Meadows and woodlands become killing grounds where claws and teeth mutilate by instinct. Fluffy, the gentle house cat, leaps through an open window to spend the dark hours prowling parks and alleys in search of prey. Bats flutter awake in their caves and fly out to feast upon victims who cannot see to defend themselves.

But most terrifying of all are those entities of whose existence we become aware only after sunset. Scientists tell us that in the late night hours our bodies release a hormone called *nocturnal melatonin* that disinhibits the brain. When that happens, our barricades against the supernatural disintegrate, and the world of the occult is revealed to us.

Monsters—ghosts—bogeymen—are they real or imaginary?

Perhaps we should turn to the people in these stories for answers. To the boy who finds his dead cousin standing at his bedside. Or to Christy, who stares through a wall of flames into the sinister face of a Snake Goddess. Or to Kit, as he creeps down the cellar steps to confront the horror that awaits him in his grandmother's basement.

In this collection of dark tales, prizewinning authors of young adult mysteries share their own most horrifying visions. A mysterious stranger sharpens his axe on a starlit beach. A boy is startled awake by the sound of fingernails scratching at an upstairs window. Unseen hands grab the throat of a girl as she walks a dark road on her way to her friend's house. A young burglar discovers too late that his victim's "security system" comes equipped with talons.

Night terror is the term psychologists use for a nocturnal experience far more dreadful than a nightmare. People who experience night terrors sometimes literally die of them.

These are not stories to read after dark if you are planning to sleep.

Or if you are alone in the house.

The drapes were drawn tight over his windows; still, a gash of moonlight knifed in. Bo knew. He was out there, standing, watching, planning the best moment to strike . . . Bo edged out of bed, slowly, quietly. Crouched, he made his way to the window and inched his eye to the crack between the drapes.

MOON KILL

BY PATRICIA WINDSOR

Bo stood in the unlighted kitchen and looked out the window. The road was a wide arc of moonlight stretching toward the black smudge of woods. The night was darker in there. You could get lost in the woods. You could go in there, among the trees, and never come out again.

"Bo, honey, what are you doing?"

"Nothing."

He knew he should move away from the window, stop being so hung up on nightfall, but he kept looking, wondering what was hiding between the trees, maybe watching him . . .

"Want me to make you some hot milk?"

Momma meant well, but what would he want that for? "No thanks," he called back. In the other room, voices rustled, his parents whispering their concern about him. He tore his eyes away from the window and switched on the overhead kitchen light. Blinked in the brashness of it. He opened the refrigerator and took out a can of cola. Momma heard the *pop* as he pulled the tab, even from out in the living room with the television on. "Bo," she called, "you shouldn't be drinking that. The caffeine's no good for you."

He slugged down the cola and squeezed the aluminum can in his fist, feeling the muscles in his arm bunch up. He let the can fall into the trash basket.

"Bo? What are you doing now?"

"Why doesn't she come and see for herself?" he muttered,

and immediately felt sorry. He couldn't blame her.

He had to go through the living room to get to his bedroom. Had to stop for a moment to answer questions about homework and setting the alarm. They didn't ask the real questions. He managed to avoid kissing them good night. He closed his bedroom door and gingerly moved the bolt. He had never locked his door before. Now it was the only thing that made him feel halfway safe.

He didn't bother to turn on a light. He lay down on the bed without undressing, looked up at the shadows on the ceiling. The moonlight was white neon. Coming in. He wished it would go away.

"That was a terrible thing," they had said to him the day he went back to school. "But, hey, what did you see?"

"Nothing," he told them, just as he had told the police. Nothing but a shadow, a dark presence doing something bad. Couldn't recognize a shadow, could he?

"But, *her*, you saw her, didn't you, Bo?"

"Not much," he said. White limbs sticking out at funny angles, like a tree split from lightning. When you see something you don't expect to see, it takes a few minutes to figure it out. That's what happened. When he finally understood, it was too late. He felt bad about that.

"No need to punish yourself, Bo," Pop said.

"Keep thinking," the police urged.

"He's traumatized," Momma cried, impressing Bo with the word. "Can't you see he won't ever remember?"

"I do remember," Bo corrected. "I remember that I didn't see nothing."

Now, in his room, he had to be honest. Maybe he had seen something, for a moment. Eyes. The eyes of the killer. The woods were full of eyes at night, sharp animal eyes looking for prey, but these eyes had been human. Thinking about it made Bo's own eyes burn. Talking about it made his skin crawl with snakes of fear. Admitting he had seen something wasn't practical. The killer might come back to kill *him*. Keeping quiet was best. He felt pleased making that decision. But at night, in the dark, fear slithered out; he could smell it. Fear of his memory and maybe his cowardice.

"Don't punish yourself," his father said. "Nobody thinks it's your fault you didn't save Brea Lynn. Hard enough thing for a trained soldier." Pop knew because he'd been a soldier himself. Knew how a man could freeze, locking eyes with the enemy. His father told him a lot of things, late at night, sitting in front of some old movie on TV. Pop talked more than usual then, confiding secrets about his time in Vietnam. These were man things, not to be discussed with Momma. Pop told him how men actually wet their pants in battle, and worse.

Bo had locked eyes for one moon-blinding moment. Didn't wet his pants. Just ran for the house, yelling for the shotgun. "He was desperate to save her," Momma told the police.

Funny how Brea Lynn and he had started talking. Bo remembered her brassy hair and sassy, inquiring eyes. Brea Lynn was popular; Bo never thought he had a chance. He was stupid around girls, tongue-tied. It was all right with someone like Melly Bascomb; talking to her was like talking to yourself. But not Brea Lynn, who cut her eyes at you, asking for something mysterious.

That's why it was so bad now, her dying. Just when he'd learned to make sense, putting words together in a sentence to have a conversation. What happened was, they found themselves walking home together on Rock Cradle Road.

Brea Lynn broke up with her boyfriend and no longer had a ride. One day she caught up with Bo and started talking. Bo fell into step and talked back. Awkwardly at first, nodding his head too much, but every day it got easier, until they were really saying things to each other.

He got used to Brea Lynn. She was the same, cutting her eyes, tossing her brassy mane of hair, giving him a quick jab in the shoulder and laughing when she thought he said something funny. But he got used to her and it was a regular thing, their walking together and talking. He even began to let himself think . . . maybe he and she . . .

It made him happier. Momma noticed. She hinted, her face gleaming and joyful. "You wouldn't have a girlfriend, would you, son?"

He didn't give anything away, but Momma must have said something because late at night, his father started talking about the birds and the bees instead of the war. He did it hesitantly, badly, and Bo felt sorry for him.

At first, after the murder, only nights were bad. Days were too busy with questions and fussing: Momma making him stay in bed, the doctor peering down his throat as if the problem were there, and the police coming back with more questions. Now days were getting bad, too. Shadows had a strange way of creeping into corners of daylight, and a bad silence was getting in his ears when he walked up Rock Cradle Road without hearing Brea Lynn's voice. He missed her and he was surprised. He had never thought he would. It wasn't as if she had been his girlfriend; he'd told the police that. She would never pick someone like him. He had to remind himself of that, whenever he felt upset. Remind himself that he was not mourning for her in the way he would if . . . well, if they had touched each other or anything.

Yet he had a memory of their touching because he had imagined it so many times. Sometimes, it seemed so real, his skin burned where her fingers would have been. He could look at his arm now and almost see the marks. His skin burned and he burned inside, with the memory of Brea Lynn.

"Your cooperation is important," the detective said. His name was Jim Falconer and it reminded Bo of hawks.

"We need to find this guy before he strikes again."

Bo was startled. "Why would he?"

"It's a pattern. They do it once, they do it twice." Bo shivered, thinking of the black windows like eyes looking in at him from the night, how anyone could be out there, watching.

"It was dark," Bo said.

"There was a moon."

"There were shadows," Bo said.

Falconer sighed. He was a tall, fair man with smudges of weariness under his blue eyes. "Nothing else?"

"What if he saw *me*?"

"He was too busy for that."

Bo thought of what Brea Lynn's body must have looked like, laid out milky white on the autopsy table, her pale neck bruised by a purple ring of death, her mouth still open in a silent scream, her eyes bugging in surprise. They'd cut up her body, looking for clues. He imagined the room, cold as a refrigerator, lit bluish by long strips of fluorescent lights, like the lights in the school lab.

"He's not from around here," Bo said.

"You know that for a fact, do you?"

"I feel it," Bo said.

Bo asked Momma to put up drapes to replace the flimsy

curtains on his bedroom windows. He had to keep the moonlight out. Momma, face gray with worry, obliged. Bo hid in the dusky room, eyes shut tight. Hoary light, like slivers of ice, pricked a way in under his eyelids.

Eyes. Could you identify a murderer by his eyes? Nightmare eyes, whorls of mad rage, wouldn't look the same in daylight. Bo took to rocking himself, one foot off the bed, making singsong lullabies to put himself to sleep.

"Those police here again?" Momma asked. "Why don't they leave my boy alone?"

"Just doing their duty," Pop told her.

Bo dreamed he was in the woods, trying to fit himself into the spaces between the trees, trying to hide. But the trees moved apart and left him alone on a moonlit plateau. Overhead, a hawk circled before diving at him for the kill.

He woke up scared. The drapes were drawn tight over his windows; still, a gash of moonlight knifed in. Bo knew. *He* was out there, standing, watching, planning the best moment to strike. A killer would want to make sure, wouldn't he? Falconer should have realized that it was more important what the killer saw. Bo edged out of bed, slowly, quietly. Crouched, he made his way to the window and inched his eye to the crack between the drapes.

The moonlight struck like lightning, and he fell back holding his head, knowing he was going crazy because how could the moon be as bright and hot as the sun?

He must have screamed, because Momma came running, pounding on his locked door. "Bo, honey, let me in!"

He realized then. It was morning. A sheepish sly feeling came over him as he opened the door. When Momma asked what was wrong, he said he'd stubbed his big toe and you know how bad that hurt.

*　　*　　*

Walking home on Rock Cradle Road was getting harder. He invented rituals to keep himself from seeing the hole smashed into the hedgerow; he didn't want to notice that particular space between the trees. These things drove him to Melly Bascomb.

He asked her if she wanted to come over. His status had changed in the school since Brea Lynn's murder. People looked at him and saw him now. They stopped to listen if he chose to speak. And although the interest didn't stay as high and intense as it had been right after the murder, he was still more popular than he had been. He expected Melly to act excited. Grateful, maybe. But she looked up at him with her usual placid expression and said, "Okay."

Walking with Melly Bascomb was nothing like walking with Brea Lynn. But it was better than being alone.

Bo asked, "Are you afraid?"

"Of what?"

"You know . . . that the killer might be here?"

"Why would he hang around?"

Bo was irritated. "Because. Because they always strike again," he said, remembering Falconer's words. He was gratified to see the color rise on Melly's cheeks. "Of course you don't have to be afraid with me," he told her.

"My mother said to keep out of the woods. That's where it happened, isn't it? We're not in the woods."

"He likes girls," Bo said.

"It's always girls getting attacked," Melly said. "It's not fair."

Bo laughed. "Girls are weak, that's why."

"Men are wicked," Melly said seriously. "That's why."

It felt hollow in Bo's chest. He remembered how Brea Lynn would give him a jab and tease. Bo felt sad and angry.

"Maybe girls ask for it," he muttered, and looked to see if Melly had heard. She was stomping slightly ahead of him in a determined way. She is afraid, he thought, and it gave him some heart back. He could protect her.

That's when the idea started: how he could show them he was not a coward, using Melly as the bait. And when Momma complained that she saw Falconer snooping around again, Bo thought it was all the better. He lay in his black room with the drapes tight shut and brooded over a plan. It had to be timed just right: the killer attacking Melly, Bo saving her, Falconer rushing in to witness the act.

He planned it for the night of Momma's monthly guild meeting. His father was going up to Swan River that afternoon to buy some equipment; a long trip, but worth it because of the price. He'd stay overnight.

"Bo, you'll be all right alone?" Momma asked. "I could cancel my meeting."

No, he almost shouted. "Why wouldn't I be fine?"

Momma didn't mention the murder. Just patted his shoulder in her hesitant, familiar way.

He asked Melly in school: "How about coming up tonight. My parents won't be home." It was the kind of invitation a girl like Brea Lynn would understand. Melly just gave him her bovine stare. But Bo had learned Melly had a weakness for country music and ice cream. He promised her both. She perked up then. "You got a lot of tapes?"

"Come up and see."

Melly would have to walk. Her family wouldn't allow her visiting a boy alone in a house after dark. Bo counted on her walking. She had to be on the road. In the dark, in the woods, he would slip through the trees.

Pop had gone by the time Bo came home from school, but

Momma hovered, wanting to make him supper. Cold sweat trickled down his sides under his sweater until she left.

He got the shotgun down, then, handling it respectfully as he had been taught to do. He found the shells in the drawer where they were kept handy. The farm was isolated. "Better safe than sorry," his father said, and Momma nodded, confident in Pop's ability to protect them. But the danger had been amorphous, undefined; none of them imagined a flesh and blood killer.

Bo slipped out of the house, wondering if Falconer was watching. The moon had not yet risen, but Bo knew the way. The gun felt comfortable in his hand, the weight of it riding alongside him like a mascot.

Before long, he heard Melly's footsteps on the road. He quietly matched her pace, moving parallel with her on the other side of the hedgerow. She was walking purposefully but not in a hurry. She carried a small flashlight, and a pencil-thin light bobbed before her. Good, Bo thought. The light will attract the killer. He'll see Melly, but he won't see me.

He realized Melly was singing to herself as she plodded along. She was bundled up against the cold, shapeless, with a woolen hat jammed down on her head. Bo thought of Brea Lynn's loose flowing hair, thought of kissing her. His head buzzed. He took a step and staggered. The woods began spinning to Melly's tune, like a carousel, spewing out a sweaty, iron smell. It seemed as if he would turn upside down and fall into the sky, and then he realized he had somehow plunged through the hedge and was standing on the road. Melly and the thin beam of light were gone. Then, so near his ear he jumped, he heard her scream behind him. She had clasped her hands protectively to her breast, still clutching the flashlight. The beam aimed upward, turning her face into a skull of hollows and shadows.

I'll get him now, whoever he is, Bo thought. He lifted his hand and was surprised it no longer carried the shotgun; his fist was clenched into a knuckle-lumped ball. He felt scared for a moment about what Pop would say.

Melly kept screaming and backing away as he moved toward her. There was a terrible feeling inside him now, like a storm, turning his blood into tidal waves, sweeping his heart and stomach and liver into the swell, dropping them down like a roller coaster into the chute. And a wind blowing, as loud as a gale in his ears. He felt his fingernails bite into his palms. Maybe blood ran.

"Oh, thank goodness, it's you!" Melly cried. She grabbed him and wouldn't let go. .

He tried to speak. Nothing came. The storm inside him wound down. In a dizzy rush, blood poured from his nose.

"Someone grabbed me," Melly said. "You saved me, Bo. Come on, let's get to your house quickly."

Her hands twisted into his shirt and she had to drag him or he would have fallen.

Inside, he did fall, down onto the living room couch while Melly ran around locking doors and trying the window catches. The buzzing was now in Bo's eyes, like a faulty fluorescent bulb. I have to pull myself together, he thought. I can't sit here like this.

"What . . . what did he look like?" he asked. Melly had come back with a cloth and a bowl of water. She was white as a sheet and still shaking, but the brightness of relief radiated from her eyes and it gave her a sort of refined confidence.

"It happened too fast," she said, dabbing away the dried blood on his nose and lip. "One minute there were hands around my throat, and the next minute you were there." She giggled, feeling safer now. "You were puffing like a steam engine. I'm sorry he hurt you." She wiped his face gently.

"Were you scared, too?"

He shook his head.

"Oh come on, you can tell me," she said. "Boys never want to admit anything. But we're . . ." she searched for the words, looking up at the ceiling. "We're bonded now, you know? We belong to each other." She looked at him. Her face went bright red and she turned away.

Bo knew she was embarrassed. It was a forward thing to say. Brea Lynn wouldn't be embarrassed to say things like that, not if she meant them. She even said things she didn't mean. Like that last day, when she told him he was cuter than a bug's ear. He'd thought that meant she liked him. He tried to kiss her, but she jabbed him. "Cute, but not my type," she said in her sassy way and laughed.

"You're right," he told Melly.

Melly looked startled. "You mean it?"

"Would I say it if I didn't mean it?"

Bo felt very tired. He hoped Melly wouldn't mention the tapes, which he didn't have. But there was chocolate ice cream in the freezer. He suggested she dish it up, and she trotted off to the kitchen like she owned the place.

Momma came back and was surprised but not displeased to find Melly. She said she would drive Melly home. When he heard the car drive off, Bo got up off the couch where he had been planted since he and Melly had stumbled in. The cushions were wet with sweat.

He went into his bedroom. The wall switch clicked, the overhead light flashed for a second, there was a ping, and the bulb died. He moved across the room to get to the table lamp, bumping into some piece of furniture that seemed out of place. He half fell, caught the edge of the bureau, righted himself, and saw his face in the mirror. His eyes. What did you see when Brea Lynn was killed?

I chased the killer away forever tonight, Bo thought. In the mirror, in the eyes he recognized, whorls of fire flared. It hurts to look, he thought, and turned away. He had things to do. He would find the shotgun and put it back carefully. He would find Melly's hand. He would hold on to that hand for dear life.

He slept, and his dreams were full of hawks soaring in a blue sky. A hawk was circling lazily, its bright beady eyes looking down before it swooped for the kill. Pop had taught him hawks, the sharp-shinned hawk with its small, quick body above the woods, and the Cooper's hawk flying in the river groves. But the dream hawk was the large red-tailed buzzard that soared and screamed, "Keeeelllllll." Bo wondered if the dream hawk got him, would he ever wake up?

The bedroom door jiggled. Momma called out in a voice full of trouble and hurt, "You got this door locked again?" Bo opened his eyes. The room was black as night. Yet he could feel warmth across his limbs, as if he had forgotten to draw the drapes last night, as if the morning sun were streaming in.

"Honey?" Momma's voice was shrill. Falconer's voice rumbled beneath hers, "Come on, rise and shine, Bo."

Bo thought of trying to feel his way to the door, but the dark was inside him, like blackstrap molasses in his blood, luring him back to the forest of night. Fit yourself into the spaces between the trees, it sang; see if Brea Lynn will let you kiss her now.

ABOUT PATRICIA WINDSOR

An element of mystery was always creeping into my stories, but I considered it just a normal part of life. After all, people are always saying one thing and doing another; keeping secrets or betraying them. Suspense is an everyday occurrence as we wait for phones to ring and letters to arrive.

Until I was awarded an Edgar from the Mystery Writers of America for *The Sandman's Eyes* in 1986, I didn't think of myself as a genre writer. But I see that is what I am, a writer concerned with the dark side—although horror can certainly pop out in the light of day. The kind of thing that intrigues me most is when the ordinary turns malevolent. If dreams can become reality, reality can also become a nightmare.

I live in the ideal place for such pursuits: an old cotton warehouse with brick walls and exposed beams. The street outside is laid with the ballast stones from the holds of ships that came from England in the eighteenth century. Steep, narrow stairs lead down to the river where cargo vessels from the Orient still move silently through the mist. There are secret passages and bricked-up cellars under nearby taverns once inhabited by pirates. Up on the bluff, in narrow houses shaded by live oaks and dripping Spanish moss, ghosts are in residence, although here and there shutters are painted haunt blue, a color said to repel spirits. Toward midnight, as moonlight turns the river into tarnished silver under my windows, the boundaries between dreams and reality sometimes cease to exist. The perfect time to write.

PATRICIA WINDSOR has written fifteen novels for young people and her short stories have appeared in magazines and anthologies around the world. Her most recent book, *The Christmas Killer,* was an Edgar nominee. Her first book for young adults, *The Summer Before,* was selected as an ALA Best Book and honored by the Austrian State Prize for Books for Children and Youth. *The New York Times* included *Diving for Roses* on their list of Outstanding Books for Young Adults and *The Voice of Youth Advocate* gave *The Hero* its highest rating. Her novels and short stories have been translated into eight languages, including Hebrew and Japanese.

A scratchy sound came from the window screen. Fingernails. Long fingernails. I felt them scratching across my brain. I listened so hard, I heard breathing. And it wasn't mine.

No way was I going to look at that window. But I felt my head turning. . . . A hand was on the screen, and a face pressed against it. The other hand was scuttling around, trying to pull out the bottom of the screen.

GIRL AT THE WINDOW
BY RICHARD PECK

"At least you'll have your own room," Mom said. The car windows were all down because the air conditioner was busted. About everything we had was busted.

"At least you'll be starting out in junior high, so it'll be new to everybody."

But everybody but me would be coming from the same grade school. Every time Mom said *at least,* things sounded worse.

"At least we'll have a roof over our heads." She geared down and took the off-ramp. We were pulling a U-Haul with everything we had, going back to live in Mom's hometown. The middle of nowhere, with a water tower up on stilts and the smallest-size Wal-Mart.

"At least we won't have to live with your grandma," she said, softer. "We'll have our own place. You'll be the man of the family."

At least she didn't say *at least.*

That first night we had supper at Grandma's kitchen table. Grandma sighed a lot and wore Keds. "I don't know what kind of work you think you're going to get around here," she said to Mom.

"You want to watch your step," Grandma said to me, "and not fall into bad company."

I slept hard those first nights and walked around town during the day. I probably wouldn't have minded falling into bad company, but whenever I saw kids, I crossed the street. I never walked past 7 Eleven. I didn't find any new friends, and Mom couldn't find her old ones. The days were real long here.

But after Mom got a job in the grain elevator office, she said, "At least we're settling in."

Our house had some renters' furniture in it, a living room couch and beds. Mom slept in the bedroom downstairs. People had moved in and out downstairs, but the attic looked like nobody had even set foot in it for years. The back part was boxed in. I slept there. The closet door wouldn't stay shut, and there were more hangers than I needed. A foggy mirror hung over the dresser. Next to the mirror a pale triangle on the wall showed where somebody had pinned up a pennant. At the back of one of the drawers was the kind of comb a girl uses. I dragged the bed nearer the window in case a breeze came up in the night.

A trumpet vine had crawled up over the back porch roof and grew across my window. The sun came in through leaves, and one of these mornings I'd be getting up for school. I was in no hurry.

The days went on forever, but the nights were short. Just after I was sleeping good one night, something woke me. I didn't know where I was. I wasn't used to this place yet, the way the walls slanted up and met at the top. At first I thought crickets woke me, but I heard something else. Something scraped the drainpipe, a tinny sound. I waited. Something thumped the back porch roof. I wanted it to be a squirrel. My bed sagged, but I didn't.

A scratchy sound came from the window screen. Fingernails. Long fingernails. I felt them scratching across my brain. I listened so hard, I heard breathing. And it wasn't mine.

No way was I going to look at that window. But I felt my

head turning. Sometimes at night the leaves rustled at the window. But I didn't see leaves now. Some shape was there, filling up the window, blotting out the night. A hand was on the screen, and a face pressed against it. The other hand was scuttling around, trying to pull out the bottom of the screen.

I wanted to scream. I wanted to cry.

But now I was on my feet. This was the time to run for the door. This was the time to call 911. I couldn't move. I couldn't take my eyes off whoever or whatever was hunched up against the window.

"Say, listen," a voice muttered. "Who locked the screen?"

It had a voice. But it was still just a shape.

Now I was by the window, the screen wire pushing in by a cheek plastered against it. My room was every kind of dark, and so was the night outside. The shape was darkest of all, but I saw all this tangled hair. A girl out there was trying to get in the window before she rolled off the porch roof.

It was a girl, so I wasn't so scared. Girls confused me, but they didn't scare me.

"Get back," I whispered, "so I can push the screen open."

The cheek pulled away. You could tell she was surprised to hear me. She was on all fours, swaying, edging back down the slant of the roof. The latch was tight, but I worked it loose. When I eased the screen open, it bumped her chin.

"Ouch," she said. "Watch it."

Then she sort of spilled into my room. She came in head-first with all this flying hair. I thought she'd hit the floor nose first, but she did a little somersault. There she was at my feet. She seemed to be high school size. I couldn't see her face, but she was looking up at me. That's when I remembered I was in my underwear.

"What do you think you're doing here?" she said in a whisper.

I thought I should be the one asking that.

"Never mind," she said. "I'm zonked."

She smelled funny. I definitely smelled alcohol. Now she was curled up right at my feet. "Forget about it," she said. And right away she was breathing steady with a little snore. She was sound asleep.

I wondered what she looked like and thought about turning on the light. I thought about going downstairs to tell Mom. Like, *Wake up, Mom. A girl fell in my window.*

Instead, I sat down on my bed to watch her, this shape tucked in under the windowsill with her knees drawn up to her chin. She seemed to be wearing a very short skirt and maybe boots. I decided to sit there and keep an eye on her till morning.

When I woke up, I was stretched out in bed, and sun was coming in green and gold through the vine leaves. For a minute I didn't remember. Then I looked for her, and she was gone. The screen was loose, unlatched. By noon I almost thought I'd dreamed her.

But when night came again, I latched the screen.

It must have been midnight when I heard her boot skid on the drainpipe. I was awake again and waiting, not so worried this time. I even grinned in the dark, thinking about her with one boot on the trellis and the other trying to wedge onto the drainpipe, heaving herself up, trying to get back in without making too much noise.

I heard the thump of her knees on the porch roof. The room went darker when she loomed up at the window. Now she was slipping long nails under the screen. Now she was finding out it was latched again.

I slid out of bed and crept to the sill. "You again," I said.

"You again," she said. "Let me in. Make it snappy." Her voice was blurry, and we were almost nose-to-nose with screen wire between. Her breath smelled like a brewery.

This time she threw a leg over the sill and stepped into the room. To steady herself, she grabbed my wrist. There were splotchy spots on her hands. They were all sticky. Her bracelets jangled, and her sweater had a smokey smell. She ran a messy hand through her hair, but it fell back to shadow her face. She seemed to stare around the room and then at me.

"What's the big idea?" she said, weaving a little.

"Are you sneaking back in?" I whispered, "Like after a date?"

"Shh." She put a finger up to her lips. "You'll wake up my mom."

"It's not your mom," I said. "It's my mom. You're crawling into the wrong house. You've had too much to drink."

"Drink?" she said. "Just make a small one for me, and then I'll have to go." But she was going already.

Her knees buckled, and she slid down the wall. She was curled up again on the floor, asleep.

This is ridiculous, I thought. But it was my last thought. The next thing I knew, it was morning, and she was gone again.

Mom didn't know if she wanted me in the house or out of it while she was at work. That morning I walked the entire town. There were no shadows during the day. It was just this sleepy town simmering in the sun. I even walked up and down the rows of trucks in the I.G.A. parking lot. I walked all four sides of the park, with the water tower in the center of it and not even a wading pool for little kids. I had lunch at Grandma's and walked the whole town again that afternoon. Tonight I wanted to be really tired.

Of course I might have dreamed her. The girl. I might have dreamed her up because I didn't know anybody else.

But I knew I hadn't because in dreams you hardly ever smell people's breaths.

That night I latched the screen as usual and left a light on. Anybody who happened to crawl up on the roof could see in and know it wasn't her room, right? It made sense to me. I went to sleep by the light of the lamp on the dresser.

Any little sound outside would have made me sit straight up, but it was a quiet night. I only woke up again because the lamp made me think it was morning. I was drifting off again when I realized somebody was standing at the dresser. By the light of the little lamp, she was combing out her long tangled hair. She was all dressed up and ready to rumble. I couldn't see her face in the foggy mirror. She could. She was really looking herself over. Then she turned and looked at me.

Her hair shadowed her face. I could only see the tip of her nose and one eye that looked bright and excited.

"If I can't get rid of you," she said, quiet but clear, "I might as well take you with me. You might come in handy."

"Where?" I whispered.

"Where can you go in a town like this? Just out. Come on."

When my feet hit the floor, boards creaked.

"Shhh," she said. "Remember Mom."

I just stood there.

"You want to put on some clothes?" she said.

So this was happening. In dreams you often aren't wearing *anything*. When I'd pulled on shorts and a shirt, I turned to the door.

"Not that way." She jerked a thumb at the window, "You have a lot to learn."

Then we were both outside, crawling down the slant of the roof, ladies first. She'd had practice swinging herself over the gutter and shinnying down the drainpipe. I followed, scraping a knee on the tin. I wanted to climb down the trumpet vine, but it wasn't there. I'd have wondered about that if I'd had the time. Trumpet vines don't just crawl away. But I was more worried about getting dizzy. I don't like heights. I dangled and then dropped.

We went around the bushy side of the house and started along the street. "Where are we going?" I said because we were going somewhere. We weren't just strolling along in the dark.

"What you don't know, you can't blab," she said. "But think about it. Summer's over, and school's about to start— senior year. You know how senior year starts around here. Everybody knows."

Actually, I didn't.

Now we were coming up on the park. The streets were empty except for a line of cars pulled up at the curb. All classics, a few low-riders, a customized '57 Chevy. Under the park trees, people were sitting on top of the picnic tables. High school people—seniors with sideburns. Girls with long falls of hair. People with beers and boots. They looked straight through me, but it was kind of exciting.

What they said I couldn't follow. High school talks its own language. And they kept their voices down.

"Who brought the paint?" somebody said, and I heard that.

Somebody lifted a box out of the weeds and handed around cans of spray paint. "Far out," somebody said.

Then they were all off their picnic tables and drifting like shadows to the long metal legs of the town water tower. From the bottom it looked a mile high, with a winking red light at the top to warn planes away. I sort of knew then what was happening.

They started up a metal ladder. Their cleats rang as they

climbed like a long centipede senior. The girl hung back, then hitched a boot on the lowest rung. "Stay close behind me," she said over her shoulder. "Catch me if I fall."

She was a tough girl, but scared now. She didn't like climbing any higher than a porch roof. I didn't want to follow, but I was more scared of being left alone down in the shadowy park. I didn't want to be left behind while all the seniors spray-painted their year across the big round tank like a spaceship above us. Either way I was scared, so I went up the ladder.

Above the trees it was cooler. I looked up to keep from looking down. The first seniors were already up there, working their way around a rickety catwalk. The girl and I got higher and higher till we were there, too. I forgot and looked down at streetlights winking through trees and out to fields and more fields.

They went to work with the cans hissing in their hands, spraying the giant letters curving around the tank: CLASS OF—

They wanted letters taller than they could reach. They bounced on the catwalk to get higher, and metal moved under our feet. I had one hand on a railing and the other flat against the water tank, and I really didn't feel so good.

Now they thought of how to do it. Before she could say anything, two guys lifted up the girl. She held a spray can, and her hands were splotchy with paint. She caught her breath, but wouldn't show how scared she was. She worked as high as she could reach, up there on the guys' shoulders, spraying in the giant, looping letters so the whole town could see the seniors had left their mark. Fresh paint glistened in what light there was.

Time skipped a beat. I was watching when her hand with the spray can swayed away from the tank. The catwalk rattled.

The guys grabbed for her. But she'd lost her balance.

She collapsed into the air, off their shoulders, out of their hands. Her arms flew out, and the spray can fell faster than she did, end over end into the night. She screamed all the way down to sudden silence, and the dark went darker.

She'd told me to catch her, but I couldn't. Every second she fell was a year, and I couldn't do anything. All I could do was scream and scream, up there on the tower above the town, and finally I was all alone.

You read about it in the paper. I was headline news and made my name in this town before anybody knew what it was:

SLEEPWALKING BOY
RESCUED FROM WATER TOWER

VOLUNTEER FIRE DEPARTMENT
CALLED OUT IN MIDDLE OF NIGHT TO
TALK DOWN FRIGHTENED YOUTH

INCIDENT RECALLS 30-YEAR-OLD
TRAGEDY WHEN SENIOR GIRL FELL
FROM TOWER IN SPRAY-PAINT PRANK

So she hadn't been a dream, but she was not real either. She'd died in a fall from the water tower all those years ago. My room upstairs at the back of the house had been her room then. She'd gone out that window and across that back porch on a late-summer night just before school started. Now, all these years later on late-summer nights, she wants back in.

About Richard Peck

Early in my writing career, a book of mine called *Are You in the House Alone?* won the Edgar Allan Poe Award. I was amazed. I didn't think that novel was a mystery and still don't. But it meant that I attended the annual awards ceremony of the Mystery Writers of America, Inc., held in a New York City ballroom. Suddenly I discovered a whole new peer group of colorful writing colleagues. It was an event that cast a long shadow. I met a new friend, Phyllis Whitney, who's been a valued correspondent ever since, and I believe that evening led my writing in a new direction.

My very next book was entitled *The Ghost Belonged to Me*. I developed a sudden interest in the weird and unexplained, a taste my young readers had all along. Though I don't share their taste for gore and dismemberment, things began to go bump in the night on my pages. I moved from ghosts to time travel in a book called *Voices After Midnight,* and more recently, computer-assisted time travel in a novel called *Lost In Cyberspace.*

Come to think of it, every novel has to be a mystery. We read them all to see how they come out, and all storytelling depends at least in part on good versus evil, and the occasional bump in the night.

"Girl at the Window" falls of course into the ghost category, though I hope that isn't immediately obvious. I like the idea of ghosts so like the mortals they once were that they pass among us unremarked. But this story was inspired by setting—all those graffitied water towers in small country towns. In my travels I'd been reading water towers for years before I was moved to a story about the hands that leave those sad bids for attention at the top of the town. Then one day the story spilled onto the page much as the girl spilled into the window of the room that had once been hers.

Richard Peck has written twenty novels for young readers and received the Margaret A. Edwards award from *School Library Journal* and the American Library Association, as well as the National Council of Teachers of English-Allen Award for the body of his work. Four of his novels have been made into feature length films. Richard lives in New York City.

"*Pablo's!*" she cried and stopped to gasp for breath. "*A killing . . . the police . . . When I heard about it I ran all the way here.*"

Rosa moaned. "*I knew it! The Bloody Boyz! It could have been both of you! Who got killed, Teeney? How many?*"

THE DARK BEAST OF DEATH
BY JOAN LOWERY NIXON

"Time!" Lucky yelled and pushed her way forward to the girl who sprawled on the ground—the new initiate into the Mobbies.

"You took it good," Lucky announced, "so from now on your name is Teeney, you're a Dos Manos' Mobbie, and you got thirty sisters who'd die for you."

"Not soon, I hope," one of the Mobbies shouted, and Lucky giggled.

Shuddering, Mousey freed herself from the tangled cluster of girls who had surrounded Teeney, trying not to gag at the blood that streamed from Teeney's nose. Mousey hated court-ins—the ritual thirteen-second beatings new members had to go through. She'd gone through the beating—every member had to or couldn't join the gang—but she still awoke with nightmare memories of the pounding fists and the pain that shot again and again throughout her body. She'd been bruised and aching for well over a week.

As Teeney tried to struggle to her feet, Mousey stepped forward to help her. Handing her a fistful of tissues, she said, "Pinch your nose hard. That helps stop the bleeding."

As the Mobbies began wandering from the alley, Lucky looked sharply at Teeney, then jerked her chin toward Mousey. "You listen up, too," she said. "I saw how you pulled back. You didn't even count seconds. And that dweeb you hang out with. He's not a homeboy. I'm wonderin' just how loyal you are to the Dos Manos and the Mobbies."

"I'm loyal!" Mousey shuddered. She knew by heart the admonition Lucky began reciting to Teeney.

"The beatin' you had shows just a little bit of what could come," Lucky said. "If you're not a loyal gang member, if you're not down for your neighborhood, then you're gonna face a court-out. Tell Teeney what's a court-out, Mousey."

Obediently, Mousey murmured, "In a court-out there's no time limit to a beating. You can end up crippled—or dead."

"Right." Lucky nodded with satisfaction. "And that also means loyalty to our homeboys, the Dos Manos. You two are our youngest—still fourteen. Pay attention to the rest of us. Do what we do, and you'll be okay. Understand?"

"Yes!" Mousey and Teeney answered in unison.

Lucky reached for the handbag she'd left on the hood of a wrecked car. Opening the bag she pulled out a long switch-blade. The silver-plated handle gleamed in the late afternoon sun. "Boxer gave this to me," she said proudly.

Mousey gulped back the sour taste that rose in her throat. Was Lucky threatening them?

Death was a recognized part of Mousey's life, yet she had never accepted it. Death had taken her mother, and Mousey was terrified it would take her Aunt Rosa, leaving her without anyone to love or care for her. Sometimes, when she woke in the night, Mousey pictured death as a dark beast who hunched over this San Antonio barrio, pointing and choosing victims and chortling with glee.

Only Paul had told her she didn't need to be afraid. She smiled as she thought of Paul Carmody, who came three times a week from his high school to tutor Mousey in her middle school's library. Tall, quiet, gangly, seventeen-year-old Paul squinted through his thick glasses and smiled as he encouraged her.

"You got a *B plus,* Angela. See? I told you. You can do it."

"See how fast you figured out the problem, Angela? You're a good student. I'm proud of you."

And one day, after she had dumped her fears on him, he'd answered, "You don't have to live where you do, or the way you do. You're smart, Angela. You can get good grades when you go to high school. You can go on to junior college. Start moving ahead by getting out of your gang."

But Paul didn't understand. No one ever got out of a gang. She was no longer Angela Gomez. She was Mousey. And all her life she'd be a Mobbie.

"Is Boxer your homeboy?" Teeney asked.

Lucky laughed. "Gordo and Snaps got picked up for burglary, so right now Boxer's the only homeboy I've got left. And is he jealous! Mean and jealous."

She laughed again, tucked the knife back into her bag, and looked at the watch strapped to her left wrist. "Boxer's been in a real bad mood lately, and the least little thing sets him off. I don't wanna make him mad by bein' late."

As Lucky strode out of the alley, Mousey said to Teeney, "Come home with me. I'll clean you up."

"Thanks, " Teeney said. "If it's okay with you, could I spend the night? If I go home like this, my dad will only beat me up again."

"Sure," Mousey said. "My aunt won't care."

Teeney was still limping as they reached the house where Mousey lived with her aunt.

As the girls climbed the porch stairs, Rosa opened the door, took in the situation, and grinned. "Juanita," she crowed. "You made Mobbies! Congratulations!"

Mousey grinned back. "From now on, her name's Teeney."

Rosa put an arm around Mousey and said to Teeney,

"Take a hot shower and shampoo your hair. You'll feel a lot better. Are you girls goin' out tonight to celebrate?"

"Shorty said she'd come by. She has her brother's car," Mousey answered. She started to follow Teeney, but Rosa held her back.

"You and I—we gotta talk," she said.

"Why? I'm not cutting class anymore," Mousey said quickly. "I made up my mind to go on to high school and maybe even to junior college. My tutor says I can do it."

"That's what I want to talk about—your tutor," Rosa said. "I've been hearin' things. Like about you and this tutor spendin' too much time together."

Mousey's face burned. "Paul's just a friend. He's a nice guy, Rosa. He's trying to help me bring up my grades."

"He's not one of us."

Mousey felt her voice rise as she tried to explain. "He doesn't have to be! I'm not hanging out with him! We're studying! That's all! Studying! In the school library!"

"Stop shoutin'. They'll hear you on the street." Rosa's glance was sharp. "Just remember, you're a Mobbie, and your homeboys are Dos Manos. Once a member, always a member. I ought to know. If you just once stop being loyal to your neighborhood, you're askin' for trouble."

"I told you," Mousey snapped. "Paul's my tutor and nothing else!"

She stomped off to her bedroom and flopped on the bed. She knew she hadn't told Rosa everything she could have about Paul. Sure she liked Paul. More than she'd admit, because she knew how impossible it would be to do anything about the way she felt.

With the help of heavy makeup to cover the bruises on Teeney's face, both Mousey and Teeney were dressed and ready to go when Shorty drove up and honked for them.

Mickey and Spice yelled and waved from the open windows as Mousey and Teeney ran to the car and climbed in.

"Where are we going?" Mousey asked as they took off.

"Gonna have some fun." Shorty's speech was already slurred.

"Aren't we going to Pablo's?" At night, everyone hung out in the parking lot at Pablo's convenience store. With so many of the Dos Manos on hand, Mousey felt even safer there than she did at home.

"Sure. Sooner or later." Shorty giggled.

The girls laughed and gossiped, until Mousey suddenly realized the ride was taking longer than it should. She tensed as Shorty crossed the boulevard and drove into the Bloody Boyz' territory. The streetlights were out—as usual—and it was impossible to see what might lie inside the dark pockets at either side. A door opened and slammed; its brief flash of light stabbed toward them, then vanished. A bulky figure rose like a specter next to their car. He banged an open palm on the hood and yelled an obscenity.

Terrified, Mousey cried, "Shorty! What are you doing?"

Shorty just laughed. "Cruisin', whaddya think? Hey, look! Over there! There are some of the Bloody Boyz' Ladyz on the corner in front of the bar."

Mousey's heart almost stopped as Shorty slowed the car and Mickey and Spice leaned out the windows, laughing and yelling, "Dos Manos! Mobbies!"

Suddenly a dark sedan started up behind them, its tires squealing as it pulled away from the curb. Teeney screamed, and Mousey squeezed her eyes shut as Shorty picked up speed, slid around the corner, and headed for the boulevard that divided the territories.

Mickey twisted in her seat. "Get down!" she shouted. "They might shoot."

Mousey pulled Teeney from the seat, and they lay in a tangle with Spice, who dove to the floor.

Two more turns rocked the car, then brakes shrieked around them.

Shorty laughed. "You can get up now. We're on the boulevard. We left those Boyz behind."

"Cool," Mickey said and patted her hair into place.

"It wasn't cool! It was stupid!" Mousey snapped. "You made them mad. What if they do a drive-by tomorrow?"

Shorty giggled. "They wouldn't dare. Haven't you heard? A lot of the boyz were picked up on a drug bust, so right now the Dos Manos outnumber 'em."

Mickey interrupted. "I gotta get some cigarettes. Let's go to Pablo's."

Mousey felt secure at Pablo's, with so many of the homeboys on hand, but her glance kept straying toward the empty bench at the nearby bus stop. That's where, three times a week, Paul waited for the bus that would take him to his part of San Antonio. Sometimes Mousey waited with Paul, wishing, as the bus pulled away from the curb in a cloud of stinking exhaust, that she could go with him.

The next day, after school was over, Mousey hurried to the library, eager for her lesson with Paul.

He was already at a table, bent over one of his books. When she slid into the chair opposite him he looked up, squinting at her in puzzlement before he broke into a smile.

Mousey laughed. She was used to Paul getting so lost in what he was reading that it took him a few moments to remember who and where he was.

"Let's see if you're ready for your history exam," Paul said.

Mousey felt her cheeks grow warm. "I didn't have much

time to study last night. We had an initiation, and then some of us got together to celebrate."

Paul didn't scold her. He reached out a hand and covered hers. "You have a key, Angela. It's your mind. All you have to do is use it, and you're out of here. There's a whole world to choose from. You can be anything you want to be."

Mousey nodded. It sounded so right when Paul said it. "Okay," she told him. "Let's get to work."

They were well into the lesson when a girl suddenly leaned over Mousey, interrupting. "The librarian says you're Angela Gomez. Your aunt called the office. She needs you to go right home."

Angela jumped to her feet. A fist of fear clutched at her stomach. "What's wrong? Is she all right?"

"Don't ask me. All I know is what the office clerk told me to tell you." She shrugged and walked away.

Mousey realized that Paul's arm was around her shoulders, steadying her. She forced herself to take a couple of deep breaths. "I'm scared, Paul. I don't have a mother, and my father—I don't even remember him. Rosa's all I've got, and she's never sent for me before. Never!"

Paul's arm was strong around her shoulders. "I know how you feel, Angela. I haven't got a mom, either. She died two years ago." He paused and glanced at the clock on the wall. "Want me to go with you? We worked later than usual. I'm afraid it's already going to be dark out."

Mousey shook her head. "No. I'll be okay. Thanks, anyway." She gathered up her books, stuffing them in her backpack.

Not lingering to walk with Paul to the bus stop, Mousey hurried toward home, where she found Rosa waiting for her.

"What's the matter?" Mousey flung her backpack toward the kitchen table and missed.

"You. That's what's the matter," Rosa said. "I heard about last night. What are you, crazy? Going into the Bloody Boyz' territory and yellin' out the window! You want to get killed?"

"I didn't know that's where Shorty was driving."

"It was a stupid trick. You shouldn't have gone!"

Relief that Rosa was all right mingled with anger that even one minute of her time with Paul had been stolen. "If you want to yell at me, go ahead," Mousey complained. "But why now? Why not later? I was with my tutor. Why'd you call me away?"

Rosa shrugged. "Because I got somethin' to say, and I'm going to say it now. Your tutor's not important. This is."

As Rosa went on and on, Mousey listened, but she mourned the extra time she could have spent with Paul.

The backdoor suddenly flew open, and Teeney rushed into the kitchen. Her face was pale, and she grabbed the back of a chair for support. "Pablo's!" she cried and stopped to gasp for breath. "A killing . . . the police . . . When I heard about it I ran all the way here."

Rosa moaned. "I knew it! The Bloody Boyz! It could have been both of you! Who got killed, Teeney? How many?"

"Just one." Teeney reached for Mousey's hand, and her face twisted in agony. "It was your Paul." she said.

"Paul," Mousey whispered, and her body turned to wood—a thick, unyielding block without sense or feeling.

"Mousey? Where are you going?" she heard Rosa shout.

"To Paul," Mousey said.

"Oh, no you're not!" Rosa grabbed Mousey's shoulders and shoved her into the nearest kitchen chair.

"How did it happen?" Mousey asked and began to cry.

"Nobody knows. Nobody saw anything," Teeney answered. "At least that's what they told the police."

Mousey blew her nose. "Who was there, Teeney?"

"Just some little kids getting candy and stuff from Pablo's. Nobody else had got there yet."

"Pablo didn't see anything?"

Rosa interrupted. "Pablo knows everything that goes on, but when it's police doin' the askin', he makes it a point not to have seen anythin'—ever."

"Pablo will talk to *me*."

Rosa put an arm around Mousey's shoulders. "There's an awful lot of hurt in the world, and you have to learn to take it. Askin' questions don't make the hurt any easier, and sometimes it causes more problems. No more questions, Mousey. Okay?"

Mousey didn't answer. She'd ask no more questions of Rosa, but there were questions for others—questions that had to find answers.

Later, after Teeney had left and Rosa had begun cooking supper, Mousey slipped out of the house and ran all the way to Pablo's. Pablo would be willing to tell her what he'd seen. She'd be no threat. She wasn't a cop.

"Watch your step," Pablo called out as Mousey entered his store. "Floor's still wet."

Mousey's breath caught, but she forced herself to ask, "Is that where Paul was killed?"

"Nope," Pablo said. "It was down at the bus stop. Some kids told me a car slowed, and the people in it looked at him sittin' there. Then they drove around the block and came back. Two people jumped out. They went for him, and it was over in a minute. After they left he tried to make it here to the store, but he got only as far as the door. Fell down on his face with that knife stickin' out of his back."

"Knife? You mean it wasn't a drive-by?"

"Nope. It was a knife. I saw it."

"Did he say anything? Did he tell you who did it?"

"Nothin' about who done it, but he did say somethin' I

could give the cops. He called for his ma."

"Are you sure?" Mousey asked. "I mean, his mother is dead."

"I ought to know what I heard. He called out, 'Ma,' and then he died."

Two customers came in, their eyes alight with curiosity, and Pablo began to repeat his story.

He called for his mother, Mousey thought. Heartbroken at her part in what probably had happened, she walked slowly toward home. She hated the Bloody Boyz and their Ladyz. She hated the Dos Manos, the Mobbies, and the way she had to live. Most of all, she hated herself.

Rosa had turned on the television news. There was a brief story about Paul being stabbed. "An honor student with a potentially brilliant future," the news anchor said. "A terrible waste."

Mousey agreed. A terrible waste. She felt the dark beast of death hovering closer. Why had he chosen Paul, of all people? Why?

"It's strange that he got stabbed," Rosa said. "Most of the gangs don't get out of their cars. They slow down and shoot from the windows, then get away fast. There's a lot more risk in using a knife."

A knife. With a quickening of her breath, Mousey knew the other questions she had to ask.

She waited impatiently until Rosa went out to meet her boyfriend at their regular Friday night hangout, then hurried down the dark streets to Pablo's.

The gang had begun to gather. Boxer and Lucky were there, just as Mousey had hoped. Lucky gave Mousey a glance, then quickly turned away, but Mousey—her heart pounding—moved in to face Lucky.

She pulled her to one side and, lowering her voice, she

said, "I was thinking about your knife—the beautiful silver-handled knife Boxer gave you."

"What about it?" Lucky snapped. She began to turn away, but Mousey caught her arm.

"I'd like to see it again."

"I don't have it."

"Where is it?" Mousey could see a spark of fear in Lucky's eyes, which answered the question for her.

"I don't know. Maybe Boxer has it. Maybe I lost it."

"You stabbed Paul with it, didn't you?" Mousey asked.

Lucky grabbed Mousey's shoulders and shoved her against the outer wall of the building. "Listen to me," Lucky demanded. "Boxer was upset and angry with this guy who'd tried to come on to me. We went lookin' for him, but he wasn't home. Then that weird Paul of yours—he mad dogged Boxer."

Mousey gasped. "Mad dogged? You mean Boxer thought Paul stared him down?"

"Right there at the bus stop. He gave Boxer a real dirty look. So Boxer drove around the block and when we came back, Paul did it again."

A sob twisted Mousey's words. "Paul couldn't see very well, even with his glasses. He probably couldn't even see Boxer."

Momentarily flustered, Lucky stepped back and dropped her arms. "Okay, okay. So Boxer made a mistake. I told you, he was mean angry. We were both too mad at each other to know what we were doin'. But it's over. Forget about it."

Mousey tried to wipe away the tears. "Paul was my friend."

"I'm sorry about that part," Lucky said, "because you're a Mobbie." She studied Mousey and repeated, "You're a Mobbie. Keep that in mind," she cautioned. "What happened is between you and me and no one else. One word out of you to *anybody*—even Teeney—and you're in for a court-out."

Lucky walked away, and Mousey leaned against the wall, trying to think. "Ma," Paul had cried out, but not for his mother. *Ma* sounded like the first syllable of *Mobbies*, and he had been trying to identify his murderer.

Boxer wasn't the one who had held the knife, or—with his police records and prints on file—he'd have been arrested by this time. But Lucky had bragged that she'd never been arrested, so the police wouldn't have a match for her fingerprints. The knife handle was silver plated. The silver would hold fingerprints, and she—Mousey—could identify the knife.

With tears sliding down her cheeks, Mousey fished some change out of her pocket and walked to the corner to catch the bus that would take her near the downtown police station. Maybe, after she told the cops what she knew, they'd help her find someplace to live far, far away from here, and she'd escape the court-out.

She wiped her eyes and held her head high. What she was doing was a court-out of her own making, yet she was no longer afraid. This time the dark beast of death was not going to win.

ABOUT JOAN LOWERY NIXON

I didn't like being a teenager. There were too many problems to sort out, too many hurts, too many tears, and sometimes too much rejection. Even the wildly happy moments were peaks with sharp, sliding sides. What kept me going were the kind, caring, and loving people who came into my world, and my optimism that someday life was going to be much better. (And I was right.)

I vividly remember my feelings, my thoughts, my hopes, and my dreams, and I apply them to the teenaged characters I write about. My characters' problems are very different from those I experienced, yet the emotions we feel are the same; so in order to reach my readers, I write through my emotions. I ached for Mousey but I knew she'd come through. Mousey was strong, she was determined, she was a survivor.

Among many of the awards I've won are fifteen children's choice and young adult choice awards in various state reading programs. Eight of my mystery novels have been nominated for the Edgar Allan Poe Award, given for Best Juvenile/Young Adult Mystery by the Mystery Writers of America—four of them winning the Edgar. Two of my books won Spurs from the Western Writers of America, and my books are reprinted in the languages of many countries throughout the world. Yet the greatest rewards I've received are the letters from young people who had never read a complete book before being given one of my mysteries. They each tell me they loved the book and are going to read all the mysteries I've written. A letter I'll always treasure came from a ninth-grade girl who told me how she hated to read until she read *The Stalker*. She ended her letter, "Thank you for the gift of reading." Reluctant readers or avid readers, I hope my stories will continue to reach them.

He placed a foot on the next step down, and his mouth became dryer than bone. The bulb behind him flickered, sending the shadows leaping. Something skittered beyond the cellar arch. Something scraped along the concrete flooring. Something big was in the cellar dark.

THE BOGEY MAN
BY ANNETTE CURTIS KLAUSE

"Don't go down there," a voice snapped. "The Bogey Man will get you. He doesn't like boys."

Kit slammed the door and whirled to face the black skirt of his grandmother. "I wasn't, honest. I was just having a look." As if he could see much by just looking. The stairs took a sharp right turn at the landing six steps down, and he'd never dared descend far enough to see where they went.

He tilted his head to peer up at her face. "You go down there all the time and the Bogey Man doesn't get you."

"I'm a woman," she answered without cracking a smile. "He doesn't bother women."

How come everything was against kids? I wish *I* was grown up, Kit thought. Then I could go where I want. And that would never *ever* be this house.

"Go play with your sister." His grandmother pointed a long bony finger upstairs.

The corridor that led from the cellar door to the entrance hall was narrow, flanked on one side by the cliff that was topped by the staircase banister, on the other by the doors that opened into the living room. Kit edged past the woman, his back flat against the door of the sitting room his mother used when she was here—his father never came, he and Granny "didn't get along."

His grandmother was tall and gawky like a scarecrow; her mouth a slit in a turnip. Maybe any moment twiggy fingers would snatch at him, lift him free of the ground, and dangle him in the air like soggy washing. Her skirt clung to his legs as if it were damp cobwebs.

Once past her, Kit dashed the final yards, grabbed the knobbed end of the banister, swung around, and stumbled as fast as he could up the precipice steps. He ran for the musty front bedroom his sister and he used as a playroom and closed the door firmly behind him. Tansy moaned where she lay on the ornate carpet, but didn't wake up. Four years old, and she still needed an afternoon nap. Why was he stuck with a baby? The little bracelet of colored wooden hearts she loved so much was halfway off her hand again. She was always losing it. He bent over and tucked it back in place.

Something flickered at the corner of his vision. He eyed the wardrobe. The door was warped and never shut tight. Kit always had the feeling someone, or something, was just about to come out, that it only waited for his back to be turned, then . . . he shuddered. The wardrobe materialized frequently in his dreams.

Wind-driven rain splattered the window, and the heavens opened once more. What a miserable day.

Kit looked out on the glossy wet cobbles that paved this end of the dead-end street. The few children he knew were snug inside their cozy houses. He only saw them when the weather was fine and they could play on the street—fine, rough games with small balls that ended with scraped knees. Kit stared wistfully at the front window across the way, hoping to see a glimpse of Roddy, funny plump Roddy who smelt of deodorant soap, shared his bubble gum, and was eight years old like Kit. He was the best part of visiting here. Kit would show up at his door and it was as if Kit had never been away—"Kit, you're just in time. Dingo says Mrs. Fernandez has chickens in her backyard. Come on, we're going to climb the wall."—all time between the stolen apples three months ago and the chickens today erased.

But Roddy would never come into this house to play. "I've got to go in, now," he'd say, if Kit brought it up. Or, "My ma says I have to play outside—for the fresh air." So Kit never went into Roddy's house, either. He decided that it must be part of the rules of the friendship.

Not many grown-ups came here, either, not to stay long, but women came briefly and left with small packages, darting glances to each side as they hurried away as if afraid of being seen.

When he figured the coast was clear, Kit slipped away from his sister's soft snores that bubbled with snot, and crept halfway down the stairs. Through the stairway bars of his prison he gazed at the dark coats hung like corpses from wooden pegs, and the closed doors of rooms empty of life. A coconut-matting rug with a sarcastic "welcome" lettered on it lurked on the shiny, parquet floor of the foyer.

What possible fun could his parents be having on a holiday all on their own? And why had they left him and his sister here of all places? Dad hadn't wanted to leave him here, Kit knew. He had overheard them argue about it.

"Not the boy," Dad had said, and it made Kit puff with importance. "Not with your mother. She's been out to lunch ever since your father ran off."

"Don't be unfair," Mom had answered. "I think she's relieved he's gone. You just don't approve of her hobby."

Kit wasn't sure what this hobby was. Maybe gardening. Gran had row after row of plants in the yard out back. Some of them stank.

"Isn't she a bit old for this New Age crap?" Dad said. "If you ask me, it's probably why your father left."

Kit could tell Mom was annoyed. "I don't know why you

say that, Teddy. They fought a lot less after she took up herbs. I think separate interests helped."

Dad laughed. "She probably put something in his tea."

"Don't be rotten." Mom's voice wavered. "You don't have a clue what it was like growing up with him and his temper. He hit her sometimes, you know."

Kit heard his father sigh. "I'm sorry. I know it frightened you."

There was silence for a few moments, and Kit suspected that his mother might be crying. He heard soothing whispers from his father.

"I'm sorry she hasn't wanted you in the house since Daddy left," Mom finally said. "But you can understand, can't you? She's had a bad time with men."

"I don't want her taking out her prejudices on the boy, that's all," Dad replied.

"He'll be fine," Mom said eagerly. "She was always a decent, fair mother. I'll make him promise to do what he's told. And who else could we get to look after them both for free? We really need that holiday, Teddy."

And Mom always got her way.

But Kit wished Dad got *his* way once in a while. Kit had never liked his grandmother's house. Odd things happened, nasty things, only no one else seemed to notice, and they got angry at him when he tried to tell them.

Like the summer visit when he was really little and his mother went to a movie with a friend. He'd woken up after a bad dream—he always had bad dreams in this house—and when he'd tried to run to his mother for comfort, the door of his room was locked. He'd tugged and pulled, then pushed and pushed, afraid in his panic he'd confused the way it should open, but neither way budged it and he'd cried louder and louder, but no one came. Was he alone, abandoned?

Would his mother ever come home again? Was he still in the awful dream? Would the cold, cold house eat him up alive? He'd screamed and screamed until he'd sobbed himself into an exhausted unconscious huddle on the floor.

"It was a dream," his grandmother said the next day. "I never heard you. I was here all night. I never went anywhere."

It was true he had woken up in his bed. But his mother would have looked in on him when she came home, wouldn't she? She would have picked him up and tucked him in. But his mother was already out shopping when he got up, and later, when she came home, he was afraid to ask, afraid somehow he would shame himself by mistaking a dream for real.

Or there was the time when he'd used the chamber pot under the bed and, when he'd stood up, he'd glanced down to see his poop writhing with pallid worms. He'd screamed, terrified the worms had come out of him. His mother and grandmother had come running, but then there was nothing there, only plain old poop. He told them about the worms and his mother had laughed, she thought it was a joke, but his grandmother's face had turned pale and pinched. She left the room in a hurry, and Kit was afraid he'd made her really angry. A minute later he heard the hollow thud of the cellar door slamming.

From where he sat on the stairs, Kit couldn't see the cellar door, but he knew it was there below, behind. Kit could feel its icy stab from anywhere in the house; his senses swung to it like a magnet points north. He tried to think about something else.

Once there had been a grandad with a cough that came from forty cigarettes a day. He had been gone for years now, Kit didn't know where. Kit hadn't even remembered him until he'd heard his parents argue. Grandad was fat and bald and shuffled around in bedroom slippers like a large, pale slug, and never said much and kept to himself. He didn't seem the sort to get angry and loud and hit people. He'd split kindling by the open door of the backyard shed in a quiet methodical ritual like an executioner in training. His eyes turned to glittering stones whenever Granny passed, and his lips pressed as flat and sharp as a hatchet's stroke, but he'd smile at Kit once in a while and silently hand him a candy bar. Kit thought he might have been all right. Grandad was always in a different room from Granny, and Kit didn't remember him ever going down to the cellar.

What did Granny do in the cellar, anyway? It was easy to tell what she did at the top of the steps, when she opened the door and found a lightbulb on the shelves just inside, or when she went down to the first landing to bring up some potatoes from the tub that sat there under the shelf of bottled soft drinks kept for "company." But what did she do in the depths of the cellar when she stayed for an hour and came back with empty hands?

"Checking the fuses," she said once. "Making sure the rain's not coming in," another time. But most often, "Mind your own business," she'd snap, or "Curiosity killed the cat."

There was a cellar window that peeked out onto the street at foot level like a half buried, blind eye. Sometimes he'd be out on the street playing and, if no one was looking, he'd get down on his belly and try to peer through the grimy windowpanes, but all he could see was a patch of bare concrete and tantalizing dark shadows beyond.

What was in the cellar? It plagued him like an itch he couldn't scratch. And the more he wasn't allowed to look, the more he wanted to.

Gradually he bumped down the stairs on his rear end until

he reached the hall. He took a deep breath. Through the door of his grandmother's parlor he could hear music. Granny had sat down for her afternoon tea; she wouldn't be out for a while.

Kit tiptoed down the hallway. You promised to do what you were told, he scolded himself, but this was one of those things that went past promises. He opened the cellar door. He teetered on the top step. I have to do it, he told himself. I have to see. But mostly he had to prove he wasn't afraid.

He gently lifted the light switch up, and the bare lightbulb on the landing below lit. It hung from the brown twisted cord like a head in a noose. Each step down to the first landing squeezed Kit's heart tighter. The closer he came to the potatoes, the harder it was to breathe.

He reached the landing. He turned the corner and faced a much longer sequence of steps leading down, down, down— straight into a wall. The cellar was to the left through an arch of brick; there was no way he could see in without going down all the way.

The bulb on the landing was the only light. The bottom of the steps was dim, and through the arch, as much as he could see, it was even darker—a black mouth waiting to eat him.

It's just a cellar, he told himself. But he needed to look to take away the cellar's power; to pull its teeth. He knew if he could only see into that room, he would never have a bad dream in that house again. He would have beaten it.

He placed a foot on the next step down, and his mouth became dryer than bone. The bulb behind him flickered, sending the shadows leaping. Something skittered beyond the cellar arch. Something scraped along the concrete floor- ing. Something big was in the cellar dark.

Kit twisted his ankle as he turned, but ignored the pain.

He flung himself up the steps. He closed the door as fast as he could without slamming and ran for the stairs, his heart a clot in his throat. He scrambled halfway up on all fours, then crouched like a frightened mouse gasping for breath.

"What are you doing?"

Kit choked, then glared up at his sister. She smiled back at him around the thumb in her mouth. He tried to be angry, but up close she smelled warm and comforting. He shook her knee gently. "Stop sucking your thumb." She ignored him.

Tansy was too young and stupid to be afraid of cellars, Kit realized, and to his knowledge, she had never had a bad dream in her life. Maybe if she looked in the cellar and told him there was nothing there, he could go down himself. *Isn't that cowardly?* something inside said to him. But, no, he replied. It wasn't really dangerous. The problem was him and his silly feelings.

He toyed with the idea of teaching her to use the camera he'd received for his birthday, but he was afraid she'd break it. Anyway, he was sure that would take much too long and he was in a hurry.

"Tansy," he said in his nicest voice. "Go down to the cellar for me."

"Why won't you go?" she asked, suspicious beyond her years. "Are you a baby?"

Kit bit his lip. Maybe he *was* a baby. "I'm testing how brave you are," he said. "So I know you're really my sister."

"I *am* your sister," she cried, apparently shocked that he would ever think such a thing.

"Well, go on then," he urged, taking her hand. "Prove it."

The light over the cellar stairs still burned. He'd forgotten to turn it off. Great, he said to himself. That trip would really have stayed a secret. He gave Tansy a gentle push. "Go on."

The steps were too steep for her short little legs and she clung to the banister as she hobbled her awkward way down. As she reached the landing, Kit had a change of heart. He almost called after her to stop—it was his problem to solve, after all—but the words wouldn't come. He let her go.

She was gone a long time. Kit strained to hear any noise, but heard nothing. Was that good or bad? Sweat broke out on his brow. Would he have to go down anyway to find Tansy, not knowing what had become of her? He trembled in a cold, clammy panic.

A scuffling rat noise made his throat close up with fear. He backed a step from the door, ready to flee. Then a curly head rounded the corner, bent in effort, and Tansy reached the landing.

Kit clutched Tansy as she reached the top step. "What did you see?" he demanded.

"Flowers," she lisped, wide-eyed.

Flowers? he thought.

"Nopoly." She shifted her gaze to over his shoulder.

"Nopoly?"

A shadow fell over them.

"Tansy. What are you doing?" Granny reached beyond him and grabbed the small girl. She pulled Tansy through the door. "Those steps are too steep. You could fall and hurt yourself." She turned to Kit, her eyes blazing. "What are you letting your sister do? You're supposed to be looking after her. Don't let me *ever* find you being so reckless again." And she hoisted Tansy into her arms and swept her off, cooing endearments and gentle remonstrations.

What happened to the Bogey Man? Kit thought. When I try to go down, the Bogey Man might get me; when Tansy does, she gets kisses. It was so typical. Granny loved Tansy and she didn't love him. He wasn't allowed to do anything. He was just a stupid boy. Granny was big and strong, and always so sure of herself. Even Grandad had been afraid of her, and Kit was sure Granny despised him because of it. She hates me because I'm a coward like Grandad, Kit thought. She probably laughs at me because I believe her Bogey Man story. He wanted to show her he was brave, so she'd love him like she loved Tansy, but he turned off the cellar light and closed the door.

It was late at night when Tansy began to cry. "What is it?" Kit asked, annoyed at being woken up.

"Bracelet," she said. "Bracelet."

"Bracelet what?"

"Bracelet gone," she sobbed.

"Oh, for cripe's sake," Kit muttered. "Where did you lose it?" he asked with strained patience.

"Dunno." She stopped crying now he was paying attention.

"Where did you last see it?"

"Cellar?" she said hopefully.

Kit could feel the blood drain down to his feet. "Well, Granny can look for it tomorrow." he said.

Tansy began to howl, "Bracelet. Want bracelet. Want Mama, want Mama."

Granny never came when Tansy cried. "I'm putting you in charge of that," she had said. There was no way Kit would go and wake her, but how would he sleep tonight if Tansy kept this up?

"Let's look around the room," he said. But it wasn't there. And it wasn't in the playroom, either, when Kit had scrunched up enough nerve to go there and search, making sure his back was never to the wardrobe.

"Cellar," Tansy said accusingly when he came back, and continued to cry.

Kit felt awful. Everyone expected him to look after Tansy, including Tansy, and here he was letting her down. I'm a stupid coward, he told himself. A rotten, stupid coward. He couldn't let Tansy think he was a failure, too. He was her big brother.

"Okay, Tansy, I'll go get your bracelet," he said, and even though he felt the copper taste of fear in his mouth, he left the room and descended the stairs.

The second journey down the cellar steps was even worse. His heart beat so hard, he thought he'd explode. I should run, he thought, get it over fast. But his legs had turned to ice, and he could only move in slow motion toward the wall at the base of the steps.

The dark mouth of the cellar entrance gaped wide, and colder air flowed from within like the breath of ghosts. No, ghosts don't breathe, he told himself. That was supposed to be comforting, but it wasn't. There was a light switch to the right of the arch. He reached for it and prayed it worked.

It did, and the cellar was lit by stark white light.

All of a sudden he felt like a fool. Besides another arch, bricked in now, which may have once led to the neighboring row house cellar, the only things in the room were some old planks raised on bricks to make a table. Kit stepped closer to make out what was on top. The surface was painted with a big star surrounded with pictures. There was an unlit candle in the center. Kit didn't know candles were made in black; that didn't seem like a fun color. Around the candle were small white pieces of something. When he bent to look he saw that they were bones. He shuddered. Bones of what? Children who'd come down here alone? No, they were much too small. Mice, perhaps? Mice caught by some cat he didn't know about? But deposited neatly on the table? A cat couldn't do that. Someone had put them there; they didn't get there by accident. Sitting on the star, they looked like pieces on a game board. 'Nopoly he thought. Tansy called all board games 'nopoly.

Arranged between the bones were scraps of leaves and flowers from Granny's garden. They were already dying without water, and he couldn't understand why anyone would waste them so. He scooped up a handful.

The lightbulb flickered and went out.

A fist of fear gripped Kit's heart and squeezed his breath away.

The dark crushed down as if he were encased in stone—cold, cold stone. He couldn't move. I've got to find the steps, he thought, in small fragile words, but he'd lost all sense of direction even though he hadn't turned an inch.

It was then the grating began, a sound like slate on slate. Kit's eyes grew wide. In the pitch dark, even darker things swam back and forth—small things that might have swum in seas before the dawn of time—things he didn't want to look at closely.

Scrape. Scrape. Screeeek.

He couldn't stand it happening behind him. But the room was cold, cold, cold, and he was frozen.

The terra-cotta clatter of bricks falling loosed his limbs—he turned to see a dead green light emerge like fog from an unblocked door. The putrid stench of garbage left too long came with it.

Kit edged toward what he hoped were the stairs. The air around him hissed like snakes. Tears rolled silently down his face and collected in the corners of his mouth.

In the ocher-lit door, a ball of darkness congealed, expanded, shot out limbs. Green light collected into eyes, and something loomed reptilian skinned, humanoid, spider-legged.

And as it slouched toward him Kit cried out, "What are you?"

"The Bogey Man, you stupid boy," answered a familiar voice, "and you've moved the binding spell." From behind the creature stumbled his grandmother, out of the bilious light, her breath in ragged gasps. "Stop, Aziel. He's of no consequence. We must finish our work."

The creature ignored her and shambled on.

Numbly Kit realized why his grandmother had never heard him cry at night. She was down here through a door with that.

"Aziel, I command you," Granny screamed.

The creature laughed like thunder in deep caves. "As you commanded that man who chased you down here with his fists?" it uttered harshly. "You were glad of me then."

Grandad, Kit thought, with dismay.

"I've been watching you, boy," said the creature, and his mouth opened wide like a closet door.

Kit backed up, ready to run, and tripped on the bottom step.

Kit's grandmother flung herself onto the demon and clung to its hairy back. It shrugged her off like a doll.

Granny frantically picked up the flowers Kit had dropped and tried to put them back in the star, but the creature kicked her aside. She howled in pain.

"I told you never to come down here," she cried. "I raised it using my hate for a man. It doesn't like boys."

"But I do," the beast said in hollow, rumbling tones. It licked its lips and reached for Kit.

About Annette Curtis Klause

I was born in Bristol, England, where I lived my first seven years in my paternal grandparents' house. I loved my grandparents and enjoyed living with them, but they did say some strange things sometimes. My grandfather would threaten to chop me up for firewood if I didn't behave, and my grandmother always warned me not to go down in the cellar or the Bogey Man would get me. Did I pay attention? No. But I was luckier than Kit, as you can tell, because I'm writing this. Those odd warnings must have penetrated my subconscious deeply, however, because even long after the house was pulled down to make room for a school playing field, it would still emerge frequently in the landscape of my dreams, and it wasn't a friendly house. Strangely, what terrified me in those nightmares wasn't the cellar, but the front bedroom or the front parlor. I always found myself compelled to open the door even though I knew I'd meet nebulous wraiths, teeming damned souls who wished to lure me to my doom, or simply a freezing, empty sense of horror that burst me through the layers of sleep to consciousness. Both rooms were directly over the cellar, so maybe this made sense in the language of dreams. The story is perhaps a way of exorcising those nightmares. Many details of the house, and even some events, are real or almost real, but I'd like to reassure my parents that all the characters are total inventions.

Escaping the clutches of the Bogey Man, my family moved up north to Newcastle-upon-Tyne, then came to the U.S. in 1968 when I was a teenager. I currently work as a children's librarian in Montgomery County, Maryland, and live with my husband and three cats just outside of Washington, D.C. The only problem with my basement now is Kitty Litter dust. My first book, a young adult vampire novel entitled *The Silver*

Kiss (Delacorte, 1990; Dell, 1992), was selected from twenty-five years' worth of annual Best Books for Young Adults lists and named as one of the hundred Best of the Best by the American Library Association. It won four state awards, including the California Young Reader Medal and the Maryland Black-eyed Susan Award. My second book, a children's mystery set in space, called *Alien Secrets* (Delacorte, 1993; Dell, 1995), was named an American Library Association Notable Book for Children. My horror short story "The Hoppins" appears in an anthology entitled *Short Circuits* (Delacorte, 1992; Dell, 1993). I am currently working on a young adult werewolf novel and howl to get in the mood.

They kept passing the beers, cracking open new cans. Then Coy showed them the gun. A pistol. He pulled it out from under the seat and held it up for them to see. Coy removed the clip and pulled the trigger a couple of times. Then he held the gun out to them in both hands.

THE BEAUTIFUL THING
BY HARRY MAZER

The boy lived on a long hot uphill street, with trees and bushes and flowers. The street ran between the Boulevard and Queen Anne Road. He and his mother lived there in Wally's house. Every day the boy got off the Number 4 Boulevard bus by the Mobil station and he walked up Taylor Avenue. Up the middle of the road. No cars anywhere. All of them at work, or gone shopping, or tucked into garages. The sun shone hard. On everything. On the lawns, and the flowers, and the top of his head. It sat on his head like ten hot waffles. *Nut pie. You're a nut.*

The houses on the street were in the same place they were yesterday. Nice solid houses, nice green lawns. Nice place to live. Nice place to be dead. Everything was dead. Dead quiet. Nobody in sight. Dead grass. Dead driveways. Sometimes a dog barked from behind a door. This place was a cemetery. A place for dead people to live. Dead people live here. He said things like that, and the others laughed. Not Coy. Coy didn't laugh at him.

The sun was in his eyes. He walked with his eyes shut. As he climbed the hill he felt something hot and thick and powerful, the wind, maybe, or something else, lift him off the road. He saw himself over the street, over the houses, over everything and everyone. He was looking down at the traffic snaking toward the bridge. At the river heavy and stiff as a lead pipe.

"Hey, jerk, look where you're going." A short, thick man pointed a stubby finger. "See where your feet are? You're standing in my flowers. You blind, or stupid or something?"

He stepped out of the flowers. He took big exaggerated steps toward Wally's house. The man yelled after him. "Hold it, wise guy, just hold it. I had it with you. Look at me when I talk to you."

He gave the man the dead look.

"You walk through my garden again I'll break your stupid head."

Bang, the dead mouth was dead.

"What's the matter with you?" his mother asked later. "What am I supposed to say to poor Mr. Vittorio? He's such a nice man, and he gives us greens and radishes. He says you stomped all over his peonies. He says you were rude, you walked away from him while he was talking to you. Are you listening? I can't tell what you're thinking sometimes. What are you doing?"

"Nothing." His hands were moving. One hand struck the other. His left hand was a fist. His right hand was an anvil. He struck the anvil with his fist.

"What's the matter with you?" she asked.

He raised his hands in the air.

"What are you doing? Put your hands down."

He dropped them, let them slap against his legs.

"Look at me when I talk to you. What are you thinking? What's going on in your head?"

"Nothing." He didn't look, he didn't want her to see into his eyes.

She said, "Be nice. Don't upset people."

She said, "Do your work and mind your own business."

She said, "Smile. People don't know what to think when

you just stand there with that sullen look on your face. You used to have such a beautiful smile."

He stood there. He wasn't going to smile when he didn't feel like smiling. He wasn't going to say yes when he didn't feel like saying yes. Coy didn't smile. Coy never smiled.

"Smile," Wally said from behind him. What was he doing standing behind him? What gave him the right to listen to what he said to his own mother? She was his mother before Wally ever showed up. What gave him the right to say anything?

Wally had his fat hand around the boy's neck. The boy jerked away. What gave him the right . . .

"All right," Wally said.

All right. That's what he always said. What was all right? Nothing was all right. Wally was always grabbing at him. All over him. Slapping and grabbing. One of these times Wally was going to get his meaty hands on him once too often and the boy was going to flick him off, flatten him like a fly on glass. Blow his head off. *All right? All right, Wally?* That's what he'd say.

He turned and smiled at Wally.

"What are you smiling about?"

Wally knew he hated him, and he couldn't do anything about it. Mom told him to smile and he was smiling.

His mother always said, "If you see trouble, walk away." She didn't have a clue. You couldn't walk away from trouble. Coy said, "If they give us trouble we give them trouble." "Who?" the boy said. "Anyone," Coy said. The boy liked that. Coy interested him. He wanted to be around Coy. Maybe Coy would help him kill Wally.

In the morning he made his way carefully around the kids standing outside school, careful not to touch anyone. He went to where Coy and the others sat by the flagpole.

He stood a little apart, on the edge, not with them, but close. It was always the same ones. Scamp bent over a guitar, a tall kid called Reggie, and Boxer, a jerky-nervous kid, always sparring around. Jab! Jab! Jab! Then when you weren't expecting it, he'd hit you as hard as he could. Then laugh. Boxer had done it to the boy more than once: whirled and then whammed him in the arm. Hurt him bad. He wanted to kill Boxer, too.

Coy and the others were talking about South Jefferson, a rival school. There had been a game yesterday and a fight broke out. Afterward a bunch of Jeffies had come over in cars looking for a fight. They parked right in front of the school, sat there, calling stuff. "You girls," they said to the guys, "you girls eat shit."

Reggie wanted to get them. He wanted Coy to do something. Reggie put his hand on Coy's shoulder. Coy didn't want it, the boy could tell. But Coy didn't say get your hand off. He didn't brush Reggie off. He just looked up at Reggie. One look and Reggie took his hand away like it had been burned.

Once he'd seen Boxer try to look into Coy's locker. Boxer wanted to see the gun Coy was supposed to have there. Coy had his hands on the door and Boxer had his fingers inside trying to pry it open. "Come on, where's your piece," he said. "Let's see it, man." He kept prying at the door, until Coy had enough and slammed the door on Boxer's fingers. Boxer screamed. He hopped around, holding his hand. "You broke my hand, man. Why'd you do that? Why'd you hurt me?"

The boy laughed. He laughed so hard he fell down.

He went out when it got dark. He liked the night. He liked to walk in the dark. The dark was like an invisible, all-powerful cape around him. "Where are you going?" his mother said. "It's dark out."

His mother was afraid of the dark. Wally, too. As soon as it was dark, he went around and drew the blinds and locked all the doors.

The boy went out. He walked down the hill to the Mobil station. It was still early and nobody was around. He went inside and bought a soda, then he went out and walked to the gun store.

He stood looking hungrily at the guns lined up at the back of the counter. The pistols were in front, under glass. He looked, not saying anything, not begging, not getting in anyone's way. Just looking. The young salesman with the ponytail let him look. The boy could tell. The old salesman didn't like him standing there. He had a pinky ring on his right hand and a look that said, buy something, kid, or scram.

The boy kept himself neutral. It was important to project a calm image. He didn't want them to think he was one of those wild jigassed kids who couldn't hold still, into everything, fingers running over things like a bunch of monkeys.

When the old guy turned to another customer the young salesman smiled at him. "A lot of firepower there," he said, indicating the guns in back of the counter. "What are you looking for, a deer rifle? Get your dad to come down and we'll fix you up."

The boy nodded. Sure, next time he'd bring his father. He'd bring Wally. Sure. *Buy me a gun so I can blow your head off.*

Outside, he walked again. It was darker now. Clouds filled the sky. A car honked, then backed up. "Get in." It was Coy. He was in the front passenger seat. Someone named Dwight was driving. Reggie and some others he didn't know were in back.

They drove around for a while. He was pressed in next to

Reggie in the back. There were cans of beer on the floor. There were four of them in back and somebody farted. "Who did it?" It was a sneaky fart. It was disgusting. The boy rolled down the window. Reggie was laughing so hard he knew it was him.

They kept passing the beers, cracking open new cans. Then Coy showed them the gun. A pistol. He pulled it out from under the seat and held it up for them to see. Coy removed the clip and pulled the trigger a couple of times. Then he held the gun out to them in both hands. Everyone took turns touching it.

When it was the boy's turn his hand slid around the stock. He balanced the gun in his hand. It felt heavy and good. He imagined hearing a noise behind him, the way he'd whirl, light on his feet, two hands, holding the gun at arm's length. And bang . . .

"Okay," Coy said.

The boy couldn't let the gun go. He raised it to his nose, sniffed it. He wanted to kiss it. He wished he had the bullets. He'd slap the clip home, pull the trigger a couple of times. Blow a hole through the roof, through anything, through Wally.

"Okay," Coy said again. He held his hand out for the gun.

He watched Coy put the gun into his belt.

"Like it, huh?" Coy said.

Coy knew. He knew how much the boy wanted the gun. He was going to let him have it. Maybe not now, but next time. It was going to happen. He didn't know when. He just knew he was going to hold the beautiful thing in his hand again. He was going to take it to the house and show it to Wally. You had to treat a man with a loaded gun with a lot of respect. You didn't say *don't* to a man with a gun. You didn't say *no*. You said *please* and when the man with the gun told you to shut up, you shut up.

ABOUT HARRY MAZER

I sat down to write a mystery, something lighthearted: *My Criminal Career*. But then I imagined a boy looking at guns in a store. He had the gun in his hands. Who was he? Why the gun? That's the way the story began: an image, a daydream, then wondering who and why.

I was always a reader. In high school I dreamed that I would become a writer, but I didn't trust my dreams enough. I was twenty-one when I met Norma Fox. She was fifteen. We didn't discover that we both wanted to write till after we were married and had children. (We have three daughters and a son.) One day we made a pact to write every day. Neither of us knew if anyone would want to read what we wrote. For a couple of years what I wrote was for the wastebasket. I didn't know how hard writing was and how much practice it would require.

In those years when I was learning to write I drove a bus, worked on a Ford production line, worked in a steel mill, loaded ships, switched railroad cars, welded steel, and taught school. Everything I did prepared me for being a writer.

All my books grew out of my life, my reading, but also from my dreams, imaginings, broodings, and things I can't get out of my head. What if my car goes off the road in a snowstorm? (*Snowbound*.) What if my parents had died when I was a kid? (*When the Phone Rang*.) What if my plane is shot down? (*The Last Mission*.)

When I'm not writing or reading, I run, play racquetball, tennis sometimes. Lately, Norma and I have been doing some heavy gardening on five acres of wild fields.

I've published eighteen books, three of them co-written with Norma Fox Mazer. My latest book, *Who Is Eddie Leonard?*, was named a Best Book for Young Adults by the

Young Adult Library Services Association of the American Library Association. The last book I wrote with Norma, *Bright Days, Stupid Nights,* was an *American Bookseller's* Pick of the Lists. *Snowbound* was named a Contemporary Classic by *Booklist.* A film adaptation was presented on NBC and in Germany, where it won the children's "Preis der Lesseratten." *The Last Mission* was an ALA Best Books for Young Adults, as well as being named by *The New York Times Book Review* as a Best Book of the Year.

But there was no one in the apartment, *no one in the hall, no one on the steps. The dust was undisturbed, the hook and eye on the door intact. I stood there, stupidly, heart racing and racing, trying to understand.*

"Okay! Where are you?" I shouted. "Who are you?"

THE HOUSE ON
BUFFALO STREET

BY NORMA FOX MAZER

It was already dark when my mother and I saw the apartment in the house on Buffalo Street. We'd been looking at places all day, none of which, my mother said, we could afford. I hated when she said that. I hated that we were poor now. A small woman with long and wild black hair met us at the door. "I'm Patti!" she said, laughing excitedly. "The landlady! Me, a landlady! Isn't that a gas!"

"Is the apartment for rent here?" my mother said.

"Upstairs," Patti said. "Second floor. I'm fixing something down here, in Mr. Sanders' place. You'll use the back stairs," she added, as if we'd already decided to take the apartment, and she sent us around to the back of the house. "Meet you there, tall one and her mother!" she cried.

"Mom, I don't like her," I said as we walked down the driveway. It was overgrown along the sides with bushes.

"Shh, Nancy, don't be ridiculous. At least, we can afford this place."

We followed Patti up a narrow, winding stairwell. The floorboards shook beneath our feet. "You see how convenient, how lovely," she said, as if we were treading on plush carpeted stairs in a magnificent palace.

My mother hastened to agree. "Oh, yes, yes," as if she had left her brains back in East Navarro, the place where we'd always lived, the place she said we'd never return to, the place where my father and my little brother, Neddy, still were.

The apartment, like the stairs, was narrow and damp. A hall led to various rooms. Part of one wall in the hall was draped with a red curtain. Just beyond it were three steps leading to a screen door, through which could be seen a staircase winding out of sight. A hook and eye fastened the door but, clearly, it meant nothing. A baby could have punched a hole through that saggy screen.

"Where do the stairs go?" I asked.

"My place," Patti said. "Up, up, up!" She gave me her crazy, brilliant smile. "Don't worry," she said, as if she had caught my thoughts. "We never use those stairs."

"So this was once a single-family house?" my mother said.

"A big, good old house," Patti agreed.

"And then it was cut up into apartments." My mother sighed.

'Not cut," Patti reprimanded primly. "*Shaped*." She led us to the kitchen, which was jammed with old, broken furniture. "It'll all come out," she exclaimed in her voice of delight. She pushed aside a lopsided bureau with two drawers missing. "Don't worry! Don't worry about a thing! Just ask Mr. Sanders if this isn't the best place."

I pressed my mother's arm. "Let's go. Let's get out of here," I whispered urgently.

At that moment, a voice entered the room. I don't know any other way to say it. "I heard the bell," the voice said. Male and deep, it seemed to come from nowhere, from out of the very air, but to be right there with us, a vibrant, demanding presence. "Who's there?" it said.

"Nothing for you to worry about, my beloved son," the little landlady shouted, sliding on her black slippers across the polished living room floor. That shining floor was as surprising as it was dazzling in this dismal place, and so were the gleaming mirrors covering an entire wall.

"Take this apartment, grab it," Patti advised. "Two *separate* bedrooms," she added reverently, as if producing another miracle.

"Ma, Ma," I whispered. "Let's go back to East Navarro. Let's go now. Right now." I began to feel desperate as I said it, and I gritted my teeth as if to lock the feelings back behind a fence.

My mother went steadily through the apartment, opening closets and turning on faucets. Nothing I said these days seemed to penetrate beyond her skin, which shone, elastic and tough, as if made of the same stuff as my little brother's trampoline. In one of the small bedrooms at the front of the apartment, she said, "This one could be yours, Nancy."

There was a long window looking out over the street, and the walls were painted a weird purplish color that I, actually, more or less liked. But then I thought of Patti skating across the floor over our heads and I thought of the voice, and I thought of a strange man living beneath us, and all I wanted to do was cry or scream. We'd always lived in our own house, but it was gone now. My parents had divided up everything, first themselves, then their furniture and cars and the proceeds (as they said) from the sale of our house, and then me and my brother.

"We're one big happy family here," Patti said, as if again she had caught my thoughts.

I turned away from her. I had never said to anyone how much I hated what had happened to our family, or how much I missed Neddy, or how much I didn't want to be here, didn't want to be a family that was just me and my mother. But, then, no one had asked me.

The price was right on the apartment, my mother said, and we took. it. "We're poor now, Nancy," she reminded me again. She was sitting at the kitchen table a few days after we moved in, staring out the window. The junky furniture had been cleared out, and from the corner window, we could see other houses, and bare spindly trees, and ancient rusting cars that looked as if they'd been parked in the same place forever.

We had had to park our car on the street. There was only one stall in the garage and Patti needed it. "For my car and my son's motorcycle," she had told me, whipping a black plastic cover off the machine for a moment. "Needs work," she said. "He'll get to it one of these days. You're a big strong girl, maybe you can help him."

"Sure," I said.

"Sure," she mimicked. Her laugh was a high trill, merry and ferocious.

Nearly every day, I thought about my old friends, old school, old life—my *real* life. I didn't like this life. My mother had found work as a receptionist in a Family Medical Practice office, and I'd enrolled in school. Every day was like every other day. My mother to work, me to school. Once a week, my father called to ask how I was doing and if I wanted to tell him anything. "No," I said every time. "Everything's fine."

"Are you sure?" he would ask, and I would say, "Yes," and hear him clear his throat.

Then my mother, scurrying past, looking queasy, would say, "I don't want to talk to him, Nance!" But the calls always ended with the two of them conferring in loud voices about medical bills and money things.

Money. That was all my mother thought about these days. How much we needed, and how much we didn't have, and how hard it was to stretch what little we did have. I didn't like listening to these things and whenever she began on that, I diverted myself by thinking about Patti's son. I'd never yet seen him. Why not? I kept expecting to hear his voice, as I had heard it the first day, hurling itself into the air, seeming to punch through the very walls and ceiling. Instead, I heard other things, strange rumbles and murmurs, and words I couldn't make out but that sounded something like hard water over stones. There were constant bursts of odd sounds above me, too, skittering and creaking noises, quick hurrying taps across the floor.

What was going on? Was that Patti's "beloved son"? What was he doing? Who was he, *what* was he? A dancer, lean and long muscled, blond hair flopping into his eyes, leaping around his room? An athlete, practicing basketball shots into a hoop over the window? Or maybe—remembering the motorcycle—a rough guy, leather jacketed, black booted, a white scarf knotted around his neck?

The motorcycle was never moved, nobody came to work on it, and no matter when I went up or down the dreadful back stairs, I never saw anyone except Patti. I began to think that, after all, there might be no one up there on the third floor except batty Patti. The noises? They could be the old wounded house protesting the way it had been butchered. Or my imagination. Or Patti, herself.

Then one day I heard the voice again. "But you don't know," it said. "I know. And it's about time you—"

Those eleven words appeared, or maybe descended, into the air of my room, like little cubes, like solid bits of matter I could have reached up and taken and held in my hand. And then the voice stopped or was stopped. Ended or was cut off. And I was left waiting for the rest of the sentence, the rest of the thought. *But you don't know. I know. And it's about time you—*

About time you *what*? It was like reading a story and turning the page to find nothing. Blank paper. What did the voice know that "you" didn't?

Some days, coming home from school, I would see Patti furiously sweeping the sidewalk out front. Invariably, she greeted me by saying in a rush, "Hello, big tall healthy one." And then I would hunch over and forget completely that I had been thinking of dozens of questions to ask her. Was she the "you" the voice spoke to? Was the voice her "beloved son's"? Why didn't I ever see him? And was there actually such a person?

This last question interested me. As little as anything made sense these days, why wouldn't Patti's "beloved son" be a total fantasy, no more real than this life my mother and I were leading? On the other hand, what if the fantasy was all mine? What if I was the one making up those words and the voice itself. What if I was crazy? It seemed a real possibility to me. I decided to make an effort to be more normal, to stop thinking about East Navarro and the way things used to be.

It was hard, though. It was hard not to let my mind drift, not to lie on my bed and feel disconsolate, and then distract myself by waiting to hear the voice again. Hard not to walk around the empty apartment, my head tipped ceilingward, listening for the voice. Seeing myself in the mirror that way, I thought I looked like an actress. A big, tall, healthy actress. I threw my head back farther, tossed my hair, and pointed my chin more sharply.

The phone rang. My mother, telling me she had to work late. "Ma, you won't be home for supper?" The words sounded to me like lines out of a play. I repeated them in front of the mirror, giving each word a slightly different emphasis. "Ma, you *won't* be home for supper? . . . Ma, you won't be home for *supper?* . . ." Maybe I could be another Sigourney Weaver.

For a few days, everything I said sounded to me like lines

out of a play. It wasn't hard to imagine that I *was* in a play, that I was acting my life, and my mother and I were living on the stage set. That would explain all the odd things about this apartment: the living room with its startlingly shiny floor and the wall of mirrors, and the red curtain in the hall (behind which there was nothing but a mildewed wall), and the flimsy screen door, and even the dreary back stairs that shook and trembled with every step we took. All dramatic devices.

Patti was part of the cast, then, too—a character actress! As for the voice—an offstage character. I didn't yet know the title of the play (*The Crazy Landlady?*, *The Voice Upstairs?* or maybe *What Am I Doing Here, Anyway?*), but, unquestionably, we were in rehearsal. And since, when you thought about it, rehearsals were actually a sort of test, it must be that when we had completed ours successfully, we could leave this place, go back to East Navarro, and be a family again with a real life.

I amused myself with this idea for a week or so. Then my father and Neddy came to visit, and there was no point going on with it. Everything was too clear. We would never go back to East Navarro. The moment my father appeared, my mother was gone, out of the apartment in a flash, barely saying hello to him, and taking Neddy with her. My father and I went out, too. We walked toward downtown, trying to find things to say. In a deli, we ate corned beef sandwiches with hot mustard, and I was cheerful and told him funny stories about my new school and how I was again the tallest girl in my class. "So you're happy," he said, looking relieved.

Later, in the apartment, Neddy sat on the edge of my bed, holding his Gameboy. "Do you like it here, Nance?" he asked in his sober little way.

"Not so much." I shrugged. "Well, it's okay for now. How about you? Do you like Dad's new apartment?"

"Okay for now," he echoed.

"I miss you," I said, giving him a hug. "Don't you want to come live here with me and Mom?"

He flinched. "No, no. I can't leave Dad." He looked up toward the ceiling. "What's that noise?"

"I don't know. Sometimes there's a voice upstairs."

"Whose is it?"

"I don't know."

"Who lives there?"

"Patti . . . and the voice."

"Is it a monster?"

I laughed, but my heart thumped foolishly. "Of course not."

A few days later, I heard the voice once more, this time saying, "You can just forget that! Don't hang on to it, okay? It's done."

In school I found myself copying out those words into my notebook. They were like the words to a song. *Don't hang on to it . . . it's done . . . you can just forget that, baaybeeee . . .* But as I wrote that, I wondered again if I'd actually heard the voice or made it up. Either way, it was my puzzle, my secret. Mine, and I didn't want to share it. If my mother and I were together, and I heard noises overhead, I would pretend I heard nothing.

In private, though, I began to talk to the voice. The fact was, I was fed up with being silent. It had gotten me nowhere. In that case, why not speak up? I practiced on the voice, or really on the ceiling. Looking up, I gave my opinions on everything—my parents, to begin with, and the new school I was in, and the world situation, as well. "Miserable!" I snapped. "Human beings are rotten to each other! Someone has to straighten them out!" The more I spoke, the more I wanted to speak and the more opinions I had.

One wet, cold, autumn Saturday night, reading on my

bed, I heard someone laughing. The house creaked in the sleety wind that flung itself against the walls, and I leaped up in surprise and shock. It was the voice! Him. Or it, or whatever it was. And it was close, it was right here, in the apartment. He must have come down the steps and pushed open the screen door. I ran out of my room, heart and stomach and feet all thudding with fury and fear. How dare he! How dare he disturb my life! How dare he break into my private place? I could have shrieked with anger.

But there was no one in the apartment. No one in the hall, no one on the steps. The dust was undisturbed, the hook and eye on the door intact. I stood there stupidly, heart racing and racing, trying to understand.

"Okay! Where are you?" I shouted. "Who are you?"

I yanked at the screen door, and it opened with a kind of creaky snarl. I went up the dim steps two at a time, up and around the bend. At the top was another door. I knocked, a rapid furious slide of my knuckles across the wood, then I grabbed the knob. The same energy that had propelled me this far took me through the door and into a dark room choked with debris. It took me a moment to realize this was the kitchen.

On the table, the counters, in every corner and on every inch of every surface, heaps of newspapers, boxes and jars and plastic containers, and lumpy piles of clothes tumbled against each other and spilled over onto the floor. I walked into another room, windowless and full of dark crouching furniture. In the rustle of shadows, I heard the breath of someone or something. The phone rang, and I stood still, sweating. Aware that I had walked, uninvited, into Patti's house. And if she found me here, what would she do? Slap me hard in the face? Shove me down the stairs?

"Come here." It was the voice. It came from nowhere,

from everywhere. "Come here," it ordered in that penetrating rumble.

"Where?" My own voice came out now in a whisper.

"Come on. Just walk."

I did, and I found another door, slightly ajar. I pushed it open. Light assaulted my eyes. The room was extraordinarily bright. It seemed pierced with light. I saw walls, a window, a desk, a computer, and on the windowsill, a monkey cleaning its nails. "Come in," the voice ordered.

For a single, fantastic moment I was convinced the monkey was speaking to me. It wore a studded green collar and a headband.

"I'm in," I said.

The monkey looked up and chattered in a high, furious voice. It had a sharp face and wet, intelligent eyes.

"It's all right, Albert," the voice said. "You—you're only half in. Turn around and look at me, please."

He was in a wheelchair, holding a dart in his raised left hand, the wicked point facing me. His right hand lay crumpled in his lap. With a loud groan, he jerked his arm and threw the dart straight at me.

I yelped and flinched. The dart plinked into a dartboard on the wall near me in one of the lower circles. The man—or boy—in the wheelchair snapped his fingers, and the monkey leaped off the sill and retrieved the dart.

"Good, Albert," he said. "Good boy." And to me, "My new toy. I'll get in that bulls-eye yet."

He had a broad gleaming face, like cold clean water, and masses of dark hair drawn into a ponytail. His eyes were as shocking as everything else about him. They looked at me directly, focused on me and seemed to see me in a way nobody had seen me in a very long time, if ever.

"Anyway, hello," he said. "Excuse my bad manners. I forget things, being up here so much. Sorry I scared you. Just showing off, I guess."

My heart was still thudding with fear or surprise. Then my legs felt wobbly and I wanted to sit down, so I did. I sat down on the floor, and I said, somewhat stupidly, "You're real."

"I think so." A little smile. His right hand never moved, nor did any other part of him, except for the left hand.

"And it's not a play."

"Play, as in a play with actors? Ha."

"Ha!" I said back, and I thought, only half knowing what I meant. *Now the curtain comes down. Real life begins.*

"I have wished it was," he said. "I have certainly wished it was."

"Was it the motorcycle?" I asked.

"Oh yes."

I thought about the crazy disorder of the kitchen and the bright order of this room. I thought about Patti and her madness. Or grief. And I thought about my parents, and Neddy, and the man-boy in the wheelchair, and then about myself. Were all of us a little crazy, maybe, a little grief stricken?

"I'm Nancy," I said.

He said he knew that.

"I live downstairs from you."

He said he knew that, too.

I didn't know what else to say then, so I stood up, but that put me higher than him, so I sat down again, but then I was lower than him, so I stood up again. He pointed to the windowsill, that I should sit there, but Albert smacked his lips at me as if to say, *Just try it!*

I slid down along the wall and hunkered on my heels.

He was watching me with those black, clear eyes. He told me his name, then, and he was laughing, laughing at me. I didn't mind. I liked it. I was ready to laugh at me, too.

ABOUT NORMA FOX MAZER

Once, apartment hunting, I saw one discouraging, mangy place after another. As night fell, I came to the last place on my list. A house on Buffalo Street. The landlady with the manic laugh, the dark stairs, cluttered apartment, and voice from above were all present. A bad ending to a bad day. The only consoling thought was that I might get a story out of it.

Transforming reality into fiction was probably what I was up to right from the beginning, as a daydreaming little kid. Daydreaming I did very well. Not much else. My writing, for instance, was kind of awful. Who cared? I wanted to be a nurse, although I was ready to settle for having adventures.

But around the age of twelve, a mysterious thing happened: Not only did I know with utter conviction that I was meant to be a writer, but overnight I *could* write. I could write almost anything I put my mind to. The kid who'd committed a poem that went, "I heard a bird named Bing. Oh, how it could sing tweet tweet tweet," was transformed without a beat into an English teacher's darling.

Another fifteen years passed. I was married, a mother, always scribbling in notebooks, always dreaming about "someday" when I'd be a real writer, when I really grew up, when I had the time and confidence, when I knew enough, when . . . the when's were endless and only stopped when Harry and I made a promise to ourselves to write every day without fail. We kept that promise, and in time we both began to sell our work.

My first publication was a contribution to a magazine column called "Out of the Mouths of Babes." I sent in an anecdote about my three-year-old son who'd said something I thought adorable and clever. "Mommy, do little stones grow up to be rocks?" I was paid $1.50 in a proper check, which I ought to have had framed but needed for groceries. No matter. My name was in print at last under something I'd written.

NORMA FOX MAZER has published twenty-three novels, two collections of short stories, a poetry anthology, and numerous articles and short stories. Her work has been anthologized and translated into many languages, and many of her books have been ALA Best Books for Young Adults, ALA Notable Children's Books, and SLJ Best Books of the Year. Other awards include: *A Figure of Speech,* National Book Award nominee; *Saturday the Twelfth of October,* Lewis Carroll Shelf Award; *Dear Bill, Remember Me?,* Lewis Carroll Shelf Award, Christopher Award; *When We First Met* and *Silver,* Iowa Teen Choice Award; *Taking Terri Mueller,* Edgar Award, California Young Readers Medal; *After the Rain,* Newbery Honor Book, Horn Book Fanfare Book.

The springs inside my bed squeak,
even though I haven't moved the tiniest
muscle. . . There's a pressure bowing the
edge of my mattress, bending it toward the
floor. Fear rises into my mouth like bile
when I hear the raspy sound of ragged
breathing. There's a click. A flash of light
shoots straight into a distorted head . . .

In the softest voice it whispers, "Hello,
Angela."

SATAN'S SHADOW
BY ALANE FERGUSON

"Satan prowls like a roaring lion," the preacher screams from the dark wood pulpit. A thick jugular vein pulses in his neck. Panting, he looks right at me. "Roaring, wanting to kill. He will eat anyone that steps into his flaming path!"

The pew underneath me is rigid and cold, and I clutch my sides, feeling the hardness of my ribs. Suddenly, the preacher's finger shoots at my throat like the blade of a knife. "People like *you*, Angela! Satan's coming to get *you!*"

"No!" I moan.

He slams a meaty fist into an open Bible. Sparks shoot from the page, and I shrink away. "Your friend will *die* because of you! Angela Jane Clark, you are a traitor, a Judas!"

An icy wind curls my thin dress around my limbs as strands of my hair whip into my eyes. I'm cold. I've never been so cold.

I try to speak. "I—I didn't mean to—"

"You've betrayed Santanna. She'll burn in the electric chair until her flesh sizzles off the bone."

Somehow, I make my way to my feet. Patches of red and green and blue light filter through church windows to stain my skin. "I did what I was *supposed* to do." I scream. "It's not my fault!"

Something in my head goes off and tells me that I'm having another nightmare. I'm not in church. I'm in my room, in my bed, alone in the blackness.

I shudder awake, forcing my eyelids apart. Red numbers glow from my alarm clock: one thirteen A.M. From the time the whole thing began with Santanna, I've awakened at the same time, every night. One thirteen A.M. That's what time it was when, cocooned in a flannel sleeping bag one month ago, Santanna had leaned close and whispered a secret I didn't want to know. Her hair, coarse and curly as wool, had bobbed against my cheek with every word. When she'd finished, Santanna had pulled far enough away to watch my face.

"Santanna . . . you're . . . kidding, right?" I could hear my voice shaking.

"No. I'm dead serious." And then she'd just smiled a tiny half smile and told me I was right about God, and that confession was good for the soul and she felt more free than she'd ever had since she did it and praise the Lord, she was forgiven. Then she'd waited in silence for me to say something. All I could get out of my mouth was, "You have to . . . tell someone."

"I did," she'd said simply. "You."

"No. I mean someone else. An adult."

But then she was shaking her head, off in her own thoughts. "I really feel better now. I don't need anyone else but you, Angela. The thing is, what I did wasn't nearly as hard as *deciding* to do it. It's like, one day, it just came to me that now was the time. Once I made up my mind, then the rest was like . . . I don't know . . . " Resting her chin in her hand, she'd pulled the outside of her mouth down in a lopsided frown. "*Easy* isn't the right word. Automatic! That's what I want to say. It was like I was watching someone else do it. Have you ever felt that way? Like your body is separate from your mind, and it just does what it wants to do?"

"Santanna, if anyone finds out, you'll go to prison . . ."

"I know that, fool. But no one else knows except you,

and you won't tell. So it's your secret, now."

That night, and every night for a week, I couldn't sleep. Day and night I wondered, why did she have to tell me? Why did she have to inject her secret into my brain, so that it hatched and writhed like larvae? Why did she make me a part of her crime?

Groaning, I try not to think about what I did next, but the scene plays through my mind. I'd prayed, harder than I've ever prayed about anything in my life. And then I'd borrowed my mom's car and driven to the police station by myself. I remember how it started to snow in tiny, white flakes, the dry kind that dusts everything like powder. People bustled in and out of the station. A man had stopped to ask if I was all right, but I'd forced a smile and waved him on. I'd waited until four forty-five before I'd made myself go inside and tell them what I knew.

Maybe Santanna felt better when she'd told her secret, but I didn't feel any better when I told the police mine, even after the detective said I was one hundred percent right in coming to them and I was an honorable young lady. "That's too much for a pretty girl like you to hold inside. We'll take it from here."

When I close my eyes I remember how the police walked into our English lit class that day. They took Santanna's elbow, pulled her to her feet, snapped handcuffs onto her thin wrists. I couldn't watch as they read her her rights; the policewoman's voice was like the beats of a drum.

"You have the right to remain silent . . . "

And then, against my will, my eyes had been drawn up into hers. Santanna's gaze locked onto mine. Softly, almost like a tremor, she shook her head from side to side, never once taking her green eyes off of mine. Without making a sound, she'd mouthed the word "why?"

Now I make a fist so tight, I feel my own nails break the skin of my palm. The preacher in my dream was right. I'm a traitor. A betrayer. A Judas.

Beyond the foot of my bed, through my window, I see bare tree limbs etch black against tiny star dots shimmering in the winter night. But then I see a black, dense shadow looming at the end of the bed like a hole drinking in light.

I squeeze my eyes tight and look again. This time I'm sure of what I'm seeing. A shape is blocking a slice of stars. Straining to see in the darkness, I make out the form of a person, head, shoulders, body. And then I realize what I'm seeing. Something, someone, is there, in my room, perched on the end of my bed.

Whomp whomp whomp, my heart slams into my throat. For an instant I can't even get a breath because my flesh has solidified into cold rock. The only thing alive is my heart, hammering my ribs as I watch the shape watching me.

Satan.

Like the ocean surf, the voice of the preacher roars in my ears. "Demons are friends of those who do evil."

And I had done evil. With all my might I try to think of a prayer, but nothing comes except *God help me.*

The springs inside my bed squeak, even though I haven't moved the tiniest muscle. I know then for sure that I'm not dreaming, that this is real. Oh, God, oh, God! I scream inside.

There's a pressure bowing the edge of my mattress, bending it toward the floor. Fear rises in my mouth like bile when I hear the raspy sound of ragged breathing. There's a *click.* A flash of light shoots straight into a distorted head. Gleaming white against deep shadows that cut across the planes of the face like black melted wax.

In the softest voice it whispers, "Hello, Angela."

Then I know. "Santanna?" I say hoarsely.

"Um humm."

"What—what are you doing here?"

"Watching you sleep. I've been here awhile."

I stagger up onto my elbows. "How—how—"

"How did I get out of jail? I made bail this afternoon. Two hundred and fifty thousand dollars. Good thing my dad left me all his money, huh?"

My head is reeling. The police let her out, and didn't tell me. Now I'm alone with the person I betrayed. A person who must want to kill me.

I swallow, but my mouth hardly works at all. My tongue feels too big for my mouth. "Santanna, I—"

She takes a cool breath. "Looks like you were having a nightmare, Angela." I feel her hand rub my ankle through the thin electric blanket. "Were you dreaming of me?" She pulls the flashlight closer under her chin, and grotesque shadows slice my walls, splay my ceiling and the corners of my room. Santanna's wild hair swirls around her head in red spirals; the flashlight beam deepens every hollow of her face. She looks like a demon from the pit of hell.

Her left hand caresses the handle of the metal flashlight, the heavy kind that can crush bone. Lying helpless on my bed, I know I could be dead before I'd hear the sound of my own skull cracking.

"Your mom's out of town again, isn't she? I checked her room before I came in here. So that means you're all alone in this big old house."

I take a breath. "Listen to me. I had to do it, Santanna," I say.

"Oh?" Her eyes widen. "Why? Why did you have to tell the police? For a whole month now, while rotting in that stinking sewer of a jail, I've been dying to ask you that question. Why did you tell my secret? Didn't you say you were my best friend?"

I'm starting to shake inside, and I try to think of an answer when I don't even know what the real answer is. Finally, I stammer. "I had to do the right thing. I couldn't *not* tell. Not something like that. It would be . . . wrong."

"Oh. It would be *wrong*." She's nodding her head, her lips pressed hard. "Of course. For a second, I forgot. In your little world, there's just the righteous and the wicked. So—I guess that makes you good."

I can't think fast enough to lie, so she reads the look on my face.

"And that makes me . . . evil. Right, Angela?" She shines the light directly into my face, and I can't see her anymore, just a white disk of light. Squinting, I hold up my hand, trying to block the beam that burns my eyes. Her voice surrounds me in the radiant brightness.

"You're wondering if I'm going to kill you, aren't you?" she whispers.

"Santanna, stop it. Stop trying to scare me!"

"I'm not *trying* to scare you, Angela. I *am* scaring you." I feel her lean closer. "You're afraid of me. Come on and say it. Tell me how afraid you are. I just want to hear the words."

Wildly, I look around my room, at my door, too far to make a run for, at my window, too high to jump from. There's no way out. Any move I make could mean that flashlight smashing down on me. Then I remember—the phone on my nightstand, just two feet from my hand, an umbilical cord to the outside world. Maybe I could pull the receiver underneath my covers. Maybe I could punch in 911. If I could just dial the numbers without Santanna knowing, the call could be traced to my home and they'd send help. I know it's a long shot, but it's all I've got.

I swallow, trying to loosen up my throat enough to speak. "So why did you come here?" I ask. If I can keep her talking, she might not guess what I'm doing. "What do you want from me?" My hand is shaking so hard, I can barely move it. An inch, then two. The tips of my fingers skim under my sheet as they creep toward the telephone receiver. Slowly, I tell myself.

"I'm here for revenge."

Now she's pulling the beam against her lips, and the light passes through her nostrils and the lids of eyes, turning her skin the color of blood.

"I could kill you for what you did to me. You deserve it."

"You mean like your dad deserved what you did to him?"

Her eyes flash. "You just shut *up!*" In an instant, the flashlight snaps behind her head and then it crashes down against the bed, hard enough to break a bone. She missed me by inches. I feel my body bounce against the mattress, and she hits again, harder this time. "You're the one who turned on me—"

Jerking as far away as I can, I cry, "*You're the one who killed your own father!*"

"I told you to shut *up!*" she screams, and the flashlight smashes close to my knee. In an instant my hand's on the phone and while she pulls up the flashlight for another strike, I yank the phone underneath the covers. She didn't see. I've got the phone pressed into my side, and she didn't see.

"You don't even know *why* I did it!"

"It doesn't *matter!* You put poison in your father's food."

A blow comes down near my thigh, and if I hadn't jerked away, it would have smashed me.

"What kind of daughter fixes a meal and then sits at the same table while her dad puts poisoned soup in his mouth?"

"*Shut up, shut up, shut up!*" A blow for each word.

I'm scared, but now anger boils over my fear, and I don't feel anything but rage for the person who gave me a secret I didn't want.

"How could you watch him die? He was your own *father!* Don't worry about your soul, Santanna. You haven't got one!" I'm sitting up now, my face so hot my skin feels pulled tight. If she's going to kill me, it's going to be with me looking at her. I'm not going to die lying down.

She's panting now. Santanna's hair has fallen into her face; strands puff out from her mouth with every breath, as if she's breathing through a sheer curtain. And then, in a voice so soft I can barely make out the words, she says, "All I want to know is—why did you go to the police?"

"Because if I didn't tell, and if you would go and murder someone else, then that person's blood would be on my hands. I would be guilty, too. I didn't want to know, Santanna. I wish to God you hadn't told me."

Santanna doesn't move. With her face cradled in her hands, I know she can't see me. Now's the time, maybe the only time, to make my move. I've pulled the phone close to my thigh; the plastic feels like ice against my skin. Once I've dialed, I'll need to press the receiver into my leg so that she won't be able to hear the voice on the other end.

"I don't just kill people," she tells me. "You don't understand. Nobody understands." With her right hand, she pulls her hair away from her face. And then, "No one else but him had to die. I only did to him what he did to me. He killed me first."

"What?"

"All I did was kill his body. My father tried to kill me *inside*." With her index finger, she draws a tight circle right above her heart.

My mind jumps. "What are you saying? Did he try to murder you, Santanna? Did you do it in self-defense? Is that how it happened?"

But she's shaking her head. "He didn't try to kill my body. That was valuable to him. No, he poisoned my soul. Every single night, when he came into my room, he poisoned me a little more. What he told me to do was . . ." smothering a sob, she presses her lips together so tight, they blanch white. She turns her head to the side, as if to keep me from hearing the choking noises that pulse from the base of her throat. "He told me I owed it to him, that it was his . . . right. After my mother died, it was his right to have me. One day I realized I couldn't feel anything anymore. He'd smothered every last feeling I had until they were all dead. No more joy, no more sadness . . . nothing. So I did to him exactly what he did to me." Her face contorts, crumpling like tissue.

I swallow as I watch the fury melt from her face, leaving a layer of raw pain. When she rocks forward, her hair falls into her face once more. I know she can't see me as she says, "You know why I asked you about God? Because I want to believe in heaven. If there is a heaven, then there's a hell, and my dad's in it."

"Santanna, listen to me. Even if people are really bad, even if they do terrible things . . . you can't just murder them."

"He said he'd kill me if I ever told—"

"So you go to the police! You got to a counselor or a friend or *somebody*. But you can't just put rat poison in a bowl of soup and sit down and watch your father eat it. You just *can't!*"

"Why not?" It's hard to see her in the dim light, but I can tell she's really asking me to answer her. I stumble for the words.

"Because you're deciding life and death. Because once someone dies, you can't change it. Santanna, when you take a life, you play God. None of us are smart enough to do that."

I don't know if she's listening to me. She's grabbed her elbows, and I hear the leather from her black bomber jacket squeak when she hugs her sides. She's rocking herself the way a mother would rock a child. "You know, after my dad died, I wanted everything new. New clothes, new school . . . everything. So I transferred to Hillcrest High and met you. Did you know that all the time with my dad . . . I never had a friend?"

I whisper "No."

"You were my first true friend. You remember when we saw that one movie? We laughed so hard, we coughed popcorn, and the man in front of us kept telling us to be quiet and then we just couldn't stop giggling?"

"I remember."

"That was the first time I really laughed since I was six. And I thought, 'It's not too late. I can still feel.' I was so happy, Angela, because before that I thought all my emotions were dead. But now that I can feel again, everything just hurts so much . . ."

"Santanna . . ."

"I was all alone before and I'm still alone . . ." And now she's crying, great, heaving sobs. She's dropped the flashlight onto the bed, close enough for me to grab, but I let it lie. I'm not afraid anymore. Santanna's not going to hurt me, and I'm not going to hurt her. Gingerly, I lean over and put my fingers on the top of her shoulder, as light as a butterfly kiss.

"It's okay," I say gently. "Really, it'll be okay."

"No it won't. Nothing's ever been okay in my life."

I don't know what to say to that, so I don't say anything at all.

With her palms, she rubs underneath her eyes. "Anyway, I'm out of here. I'm going to skip bail and run. I'm taking a bus, and heading up north so I can just—disappear. Maybe I can start a new life. God knows I hate the one I've had."

Breathing in deeply, Santanna straightens. Her head rolls back so that she's looking straight at the ceiling, her mouth just slightly open. A sigh that is deeper than any I've ever heard escapes from her open throat. "You think you know what you'd do if you were me. You think you would have gone to the police, and they would have come and taken the bad guy away and made it all better. And you know what?"

"What?" I ask softly.

"I want you to keep on believing that. Maybe, if enough people believe good things, maybe that will make it true."

She's on her feet now. "Good-bye, Angela." The flashlight clicks off, and like a shadow, she's gone.

Outside my window I hear her footsteps scuff the driveway, or is it the last of the dead leaves rattling in the wind? I feel the phone pressing into my thigh, hot now, like my flesh, and I know what I have to do. I have to call the police and tell them a murderer is escaping. I need to pick up the phone and dial because she's a killer and she's getting away. It's the right thing to do. I pull the top of the Trimline from underneath the covers and bring it up to my eyes. The lights from buttons glow neon yellow, each one cut in the middle by a stark black number. My finger slides across the keypad to the nine. The tone makes me wince. Now my finger hesitates over the number one. I take a breath and press it down. One more time. I need to press the key one more time. My finger hovers . . . and then I set the receiver back in its cradle. I shove the phone away from me. It hits my floor and clatters across the hard wood.

I can't do it. I don't know what's changed, Santanna, me, or both, but I can't make the call, not now, not ever. Staring into the blackness, I hear the computer voice as it tells me to *please hang up and try again*. I don't move when the beep beep beep cuts through the stillness, like the anxious beat of a heart monitor, until it quiets to a gentle hum.

"So we have a secret, Santanna," I whisper to the ceiling. "You and me and God."

Santanna will never really get away with it. She'll carry

what she did to her father for the rest of her life, and it'll haunt her like a demon. In a way, she'll always be locked up, no matter how far she runs.

For what's left of the night I lie there, staring out my window. I watch the sky shift from black to deep purple, see the stars turn to water before they fade into the morning. I wonder how far Satanna's gone. I wonder if the police will catch her. Maybe she'll be arrested at some bus station, and when they find out she was here, the detectives will come to me and say, "Why didn't you call us, Angela? Santanna is a killer. Why didn't you turn her in?"

And I'll say simply, "I always try to do the right thing."

About Alane Ferguson

What would I do if a friend told me she'd murdered some-one and gotten away with it? That's the question I asked myself immediately after hearing the real-life story of a girl who confessed that she'd poisoned her own father. But this confession wasn't given to the police, it was whispered into the ear of the killer's very best friend. In the end, the terrible secret shattered both girls' lives.

The girl who was entrusted with this grisly confidence had to make a choice: to tell, or to become an unwilling part of the conspiracy. And so I asked myself, what would I do if that were me? Would I tell the police? If I didn't come forward, and if my friend murdered again, would the new victim's blood be on my hands? What is true friendship? Are there really secrets too big to keep?

Because my own best friend, Savannah Anderson, was mur-dered by a serial killer (whom the police dubbed the Orange County Slayer), I've often thought of the issues surrounding the death of one person at the hands of another. I've won-dered if Savannah's killer ever confessed his own demons to another soul. And I've wondered if he had, and that other per-son had come forward, could my friend have been saved? Is there ever a reason good enough to remain silent . . .

ALANE FERGUSON's first novel, *Show Me the Evidence*, was the winner of the 1990 Edgar Allan Poe Award, the Belgium Children's Choice Book Award, the International Reading Association's Young Adults' Choice, The New York Public Library's Books for the Teen Age, 1990, and ALA Recommended Book for Reluctant Young Adult Readers. *Overkill*, her second mystery novel, was also an ALA Recommended Book for Reluctant Young Adult Readers and the New York Public Library's Books for the Teen Age, 1993. Her newest mystery, *Poison*, was a nominee for the 1995 Edgar Allan Poe Award. Alane Ferguson is also the author of numerous middle grade novels, as well as picture books. The author lives in Sandy, Utah, with her husband Ron, and her three children, Kristin (19), Daniel (12), and Katherine (10).

"*What is it, what's to do?*" she demanded.

And was answered by a frantic cry from the floor, somewhere near the bed.

"*Murder,* murder, *they're killing me, they're digging their claws into my* brain!"

THE MONKEY'S WEDDING
BY JOAN AIKEN

FAMOUS PICTURE DISCOVERED AFTER FIFTY YEARS! said the headlines. *The Monkey's Wedding* located at last.

And underneath, in smaller type, the newspaper stories told how Jan Invach's celebrated, almost legendary picture of a street scene in the town of Foçjau, the people in the street, the man running with the dove, the girl with red hair, and the high-arched, seven-hundred-year-old bridge over the river Foç—well, anyway, this wonderful picture, which had sold on its first showing for eight thousand pounds, and that was in 1939, and soon after in World War II, it had been lost in France, looted by the Germans, taken to Berlin, looted again by the Russians, taken to Moscow, lost again, and had only recently come to light after having been smuggled over the frontier between Kikl and Soubctavia—well, this historic picture had now been reclaimed by its painter, Jan Invach, who had made a special journey to Soubctavia (now torn asunder, alas, by disastrous civil war and dire internal strife) to identify the painting, of which, since it was lost, he had done two more versions from memory, but had always wished to recover the original if it were possible to do so. *The Monkey's Wedding*, of course, in colloquial idiom, means a scene with sunshine viewed through rain, or rain seen through the sun's rays. Jan Invach painted the original picture at the age of eighteen. Now in his seventies, but hale and well, he is world-famous and his pictures fetch astronomic sums. What *The*

Monkey's Wedding first version must be worth now is almost impossible to compute . . .

Old Mrs. Invach sniffed, reading this news story as related by various daily papers while drinking elderflower tea in her large, dark, shabby, cluttered Hampstead kitchen.

"Untold millions, ha! Money's not worth the paper it's printed on these days. In 1939, with what that picture sold for, you could have bought a couple of islands. Now, you couldn't buy a tub of ice cream. And if you could, it wouldn't be worth eating."

Old Mrs. Invach, now in her nineties, talked to herself all day long. It was a family habit. Her son did it as he painted his pictures. Sitters for portraits were frequently disconcerted, and sometimes tried to respond, but he paid them no heed. The Tate Gallery had a tape of the entire monologue that had accompanied his charcoal drawing of the Duchess of Cambridge.

Mrs. Invach switched on the TV news, and sat muttering and mumbling at the newscaster.

"United Nations monitoring a cease-fire in Soubctavia. Ha! That won't last long! *I* know those Soubs and those Dobrindjans—they'll be at each other's throats again in thirty-six hours."

There were shots of the beautiful old town of Foçjau and the celebrated bridge—now shattered beyond repair, nothing left of its seven-hundred-year-old curve but some dangling fragments of masonry.

"If they ever want to rebuild it, they'll need to look at Jan's picture," muttered Mrs. Invach. "But will that time ever come? I very much doubt it."

"The world-famous painter Jan Invach is in the town of Foçjau at present, on a mission to rescue his legendary picture *The Monkey's Wedding* which was recently discovered not far away in a barn, just over the border in the province of Kikl. An unknown sum had been paid for its ransom by an unknown Japanese millionaire who wished to return the picture to the man who painted it. He plans to donate it to the National Gallery in London, but before that he intends to effect various necessary repairs to the canvas, which was discovered leaning against a damp wall behind a heap of turnips . . .

"A threatened strike of dentists has been averted by the junior Health Minister . . ." cop 4

The doorbell rang, and Mrs. Invach switched off the weather forecast and shuffled into the front hall, muttering and grumbling. It took her a while to undo various bolts and Chubb locks; the chain she left on while she peered around the crack of the door into the face of a lad of perhaps eighteen who wore a brand-new tartan cap and carried a shiny briefcase.

"Evening, Missus!" he said with cheerful confidence. "I represent McCustody home security systems and burglar alarms. I'll be happy to survey your home here and now, and give you a free estimate for our complete scheme of protection—"

He was studying her intently all the time as he spoke, and she, meanwhile, was subjecting him to an equally gimlet-eyed scrutiny. Mrs. Invach was a rugged-looking old lady with hair and skin almost completely pale, bleached as desert grass; her scanty hair was pulled straight back into a knot, she wore a rough woolen monk's robe, and her eyes were like flint arrowheads.

"Why should you think I haven't a security system already?" she demanded tartly.

"I checked around with all the main companies before I came." The boy gave her a brash grin. "None had your name on their lists. And, just now, you'll be wanting a fair deal of extra security—won't you?"

"What do you mean by that?" she snapped.

Somehow, during this exchange, she had moved back a step or two, and he had contrived to twitch off the door-chain and enter her front hall, which he glanced around, taking rapid stock of its solid walls and massive Victorian mahogany stair-rail. When he raised his eyes to the upper level, he drew in a sharp breath, for there, facing each other across the landing, were two Jan Invach paintings, explosions of dark, brilliant, menacing color.

"When your son comes back to England with that picture," he said with a candid grin.

"What do you know about my son?" the old woman demanded.

"I read the papers, don't I? My firm expects me to scout about, finding likely customers. You want all the art thieves in Europe making a beeline for this house? Now we can put you in a foolproof, sabotage-resistant, easy-care system *exactly* suited to your needs—" he tapped his fat briefcase— "in less than twenty-four hours you can have it all installed and be able to snap your fingers at bandits."

He snapped his fingers.

"All I need is to take a look at your ground-floor rooms . . . " He glanced with unconcealed inquisitiveness towards the two doors—drawing room, dining room, most probably, which opened on either side of the hall, and the third door at the rear, leading, no doubt, to the kitchen regions.

But Mrs. Invach wasn't having any.

"No. Thank you, young man. *Not* today. Not any day, for that matter. I do not need your security system, or anybody's. I take my own measures. Thank you. Good day."

She pushed him inexorably back through the crack of the door.

"You'll be sorry—really sorry! You don't know what a

bad mistake you are making," he called back through the crack.

"I make my own mistakes!" she shouted. After relocking the door behind him, she moved slowly towards the kitchen to prepare her evening meal. On the dark blue kitchen walls above the dirty braided rug glimmered a half dozen more Invach canvases, some framed, some unframed. The kitchen was roomy and dim, with a potbellied iron stove, a large old refrigerator, and a small Victorian bureau used by Mrs. Invach as a bar, containing bottles of vodka, bourbon, bitters, wines, and liqueurs. Racks of tapes hung on one wall, and the old woman switched on a player as she mixed herself a drink, cut up onions, and chopped spinach.

Her son's voice filled the room, arguing with itself in a low, collected murmuring monologue just louder than a whisper.

"Sky's getting darker now—float of azure mist against distant hill—smoke rolling up from somebody's bonfire—'commentary-driving' they used to make you do it on those advanced motor courses, opposing traffic, hazards, mirror, say I'm doing a moderate thirty in a built-up area—lemon-green in the ash flowers, splash of white on top of that mushroom shape, loose flecks of black in the angle—now there's a woman walking along, throws up her feet like serifs on capital letters, put her in, back like a stick of celery just what I need, a vertical up there hooking into the sky—great wallop of white cloud like a walrus's back arching up over the housetops—houses climbing the hill make a dark diagonal—something coming toward me, green on lighter green—"

Mrs. Invach sighed and dropped her vegetables into a pot to sizzle and frizzle in oil. Later she would add milk and stock. She lived almost entirely on vegetable soup. Up above her in the gloom she heard a faint keening whistle.

"All right, all right," she grumbled. "I got your bones, don't worry."

Some of the bones had gone into her soup stock, but some remained raw as a snack for Alpha and Beta, the two peregrines, who had their own entry in a round, east-facing window upstairs, their home in a dark, cobwebby loft.

"Texture very important," said her son's voice. "And everything must be three-dimensional. Except the sky? Even the sky? Can you have three-dimensional sky? Don't see why not. What else is there besides up, across, and sideways? Before? After? Alongside? Next door? Now, in that mass of black a red sun hanging—it needs to pierce the black like blood soaking through a bandage . . . black must have texture, though, solid as rock all crisscrossed and veined with seams of fine, very dark brown . . . but the red comes clear through, round as a penny . . ."

Presently Mrs. Invach went upstairs to bed. Her bedroom was virtually empty, save for the large flat bed, like a platform, covered by a Turkish rug and cushions. Inside the bedroom door a massive vacuum cleaner was attached to the wall by a tangle of tubes and cords. On three walls, more of Jan's pictures, severe, complex, and luminous. The fourth wall held two huge windows, oblong against blackness, with wide, low sills.

Before her final descent into bed, Mrs. Invach regularly devoted the last hour of her day to what she called "searching."

The first stage was a physical search for all the items she had mislaid in the course of the day, in the course of the week. She lived in permanent arrears, carried out a nonstop quest, for her scarf, her spectacles, the gas bill, the book she was reading, another book now due for return to the library, a letter from cousin Anatol in Buffalo, her favorite pen, her membership card of the Foreigners' Forum, an advertisement for Arthritis Oil, a newspaper clipping she intended to send to her niece in Tokyo, a packet of plant food, a scented candle somebody had given her that was supposed to be a specific against insomnia, an invitation to a private view of watercolors, a letter long overdue for an answer from a man who wanted to write her biography, and keys, dozens of keys. . . . All these things needed to be found, and some of them, perhaps, would be found, but then, most probably, lost again in the hunt for others that were, or seemed, more instantly necessary.

And some would never be found.

The retrieval of even one, even two, lost possessions would quickly operate a change of gear in Mrs. Invach's mental workings: she would steady down, restlessness replaced by an inward-looking process; she sat herself comfortably on the broad bedroom windowsill where found objects were first laid (before being lost again) and began to operate her majestic memory. The contents of her mind, a huge lumber-room containing ninety years of accumulated events, were like an archaeologist's treasure heap, like the buried cities of Troy. Into this heap she plunged a scoop and dragged out whatever she fancied. If only it could be so with the things in the house!

"Nineteen forty-one, Jan and I walking across Europe, dodging the Germans. The night we spent with Professor Crzvdgrad and talked about rainbows—then next day they caught him, arrested him, and put him in a camp. We heard of his death four years later. . . . And it was on that walk that Jan painted the first *Monkey's Wedding*; he carried it with him, rolled in his sleeping bag. I remember the man with the dove. . . ."

The telephone rang, insistently. Sifting back into shadows,

the man with the dove returned to the year '41. Mrs. Invach had a phone extension on the bedroom windowsill. She picked up the receiver.

"Mrs. Ludmilla Invach? This is Sam Stoles of the *Morning Post* art page. I understand you were with your son, Jan, when he painted the original *Monkey's Wedding* picture—when you were escaping from German-occupied Europe?"

"I was with him," growled Mrs. Invach. She detested newspapers and newspapermen, but knew that it was not wise to antagonize them.

"You watched him paint the picture?"

"Oh, not all the time. It took him six days, you know."

"Six days of great danger when the Germans were coming closer and closer."

"You don't have to tell *me* that, young man."

"You have heard that he has retrieved the picture—is coming back to this country with it?"

"So the gossip runs—"

"Will he be coming to your house?"

"Possibly. I have not yet been informed. Perhaps he will take it straight to the National Gallery—to work on it there—"

So said Mrs. Invach, but in fact she believed that Jan would come to Hampstead. Why not? In between his huge travels he generally did use her big top-floor studio.

"Your son has a home of his own? Is he married? Children?"

"No. Never. None."

"And his father? Your—husband?"

"Gone. Long ago. He remained behind in Dobrin. Died, I heard, when Jan was ten."

These facts came from Mrs. Invach like dregs of juice from an already-squeezed lemon.

"Young man, I am at this time expecting my son to telephone me. I would be much obliged if you would hang up. I can tell you *no* more. Good night."

"Good night, Mrs. Invach."

She was *not* expecting her son to call, but in fact two minutes later the phone did ring again, a foreign operator asking a question.

"Pirhda?—Ach—Jan, it is you! From where do you call?"

"Mother? I'm in Foçjau—in a callbox. Listen: things are quite rough here. Can you hear the gunfire?"

She could, like a spatter of hail against the windows. But it was June . . .

"They have snipers in the hills around, firing into the town, teasing the inhabitants . . . They watch a woman go to the well with her pail, they wait until she has returned within three steps of her front door, then drill a row of holes into the pail . . ."

That was so like Jan, he paid heed only to the inessentials, the small details.

"But did you get the picture? When can you come back here?"

"Yes, I got the picture. Mother, do you remember a girl called Amalçja? In Foçjau?"

Down plunged the accurate probe into the mass of memories.

"Certainly I remember her." A girl with brilliant red hair and a brilliant razor-sharp mind. A combative, scrutinizing girl. A rival. "She died in a camp, we heard."

"No," said Jan. "She did not die. Not then, not there."

"So? Is that so?" Mrs. Invach playing for time.

"You were wrong when you told me that, Mother."

Did he mean *wrong* in the moral sense, or merely mistaken?

She said, evasively, "So many untrue stories ran about at that time. You have news of her?"

"No, only that she did not die. She—"

"But when will you come back?"

"Tomorrow, if I can make it to the U.N. Headquarters. If we can make it to the airport. They call that road Suicides' Mile."

"I wish that you were here, *now*," she said, sounding, suddenly, her full age, and pitiful. "*Why* did you have to go back for that picture? It was lost for so long—"

"It was part of me. I needed to take another look. Goodbye, Mother!"

"I shall see you back in London!" she called loudly, but the line had already gone dead, and she was left with the empty receiver in her hand, staring across a wide, dangerous distance in which a red-haired girl—not handsome, no, but with a keen scornful face like the prow of a ship—a red-headed girl had laughed and argued and teased, and made far too strong a bid for her son Jan's attention.

Next day Mrs. Invach got up very late and shuffled around the house all day in her threadbare monk's robe and Turkish slippers. For once, the house was quite silent. She had not the heart to talk to herself, she did not dare play tapes of Jan's voice. That would be to tempt the wicked spirits. And there were far too many of those about the world, too many and too strong. Some of them inside herself.

What had happened to that girl Amalçja? Where had she gone? What had she done with herself?

We were happy, thought Mrs. Invach, just the two of us, until she came along.

Some men—the great artists—are better alone. They do not need women. Art is enough for them. Jan was one of that sort.

Was? What do I mean by *was?* Perhaps he is coming into Heathrow at this moment.

But at teatime—not that Mrs. Invach drank tea, she drank vodka with homemade elderflower cordial, made from her own backyard trees—the Foreign Office South-Eastern Europe Cultural and Educational Department rang her.

"Mrs. Invach?"

"Yes," she croaked, knowing already.

"We are sorry to bring you bad news—"

"Yes?"

"Your son—the painter Jan Invach—he has been very seriously wounded, on his way to the airport at Foçjau. He was flown out—to Ancona—where he is in a hospital, in intensive care—but, hopes for his survival are not high. We think it best to warn you—"

"Should I go there? To Ancona? Should I get on a plane?"

"No, no, Mrs. Invach, we cannot advise that. No, but what we are calling to inquire is—"

"Yes? *Yes?*"

"The painting your son went to verify—to establish—to authenticate—"

"So?"

"He had it with him when he was—it has been dispatched to this country. There were some bullet holes and a tear—nothing too bad—"

"The picture is okay, but my son is dying?" sourly said Mrs. Invach.

"The picture will be delivered to you *very shortly,* Mrs. Invach. This was at your son's express request. He would not rest until he was assured that it was on its way. We would like to arrange for police protection of your house during the next five days, Mrs. Invach—we have made arrangements with the art and antiques squad at Scotland Yard—until acknowledgment of the legal ownership of the picture has been definitely established—"

"*Established?*" she spat.

"It is a matter for knotty legal consideration, Mrs. Invach. The Japanese buyer who acquired it—he made it plain that his intention was to give it to your son—give it back to him—"

"*Give* it back? But my son painted it in the first place. It was his, his own work, his property—"

"No, Mrs. Invach, for he sold it—the original purchaser is lost, unavailable. But the question is, did the Japanese gentleman have the right to buy it—for it had been stolen, several times—"

"It belongs to my son!"

"And suppose your son should not survive, Mrs. Invach?"

She said: "Excuse me. Somebody is ringing at my front doorbell . . . I must hang up."

"*Mrs. Invach!*"

She put back the receiver on its rest and pattered to the front door. There a delivery man handed her a rolled-up package three meters long, lavishly wrapped in plastic padding, secured with heavy tape and gaudy labels and numerous lead seals.

She was asked to sign in nine different places.

The delivery man drove off, having first subjected the house, in its untidy garden, to a long, careful scrutiny.

Mrs. Invach shut, bolted, and chained the front door. Carrying the package through to the kitchen, she began tussling with the formidable wrappings. Kitchen scissors and a razor blade at last defeated them. She took the rolled canvas into what had once been the dining room. Now the huge mahogany table, bloomed over with damp, held old maps, boxes of family papers, rolls of patchwork, an old-fashioned windup gramophone, and a Singer sewing machine, period 1890.

All these things were thrust onto the floor, and the canvas unrolled, weighted down at the corners with large lumps of rock brought home from the Dolomite Mountains.

The Monkey's Wedding blazed up at the ceiling, and Mrs. Invach stood, hands on hips, a crease between her brows, estimating what must be done to it. The bullet holes, there and there, yes, a dark stain of blood, and patches of damp—from the turnip heap, probably—and a tear, quite a bad tear at one corner . . .

Somberly, lower lip out-thrust, frowning still, she left the room, head bent. She locked the dining room door and put the key in her skirt pocket. Went to watch the six-o'clock news.

"The well-known painter, Jan Invach, died of bullet wounds this afternoon in a military hospital in Ancona after a successful bid to rescue his world-famous picture, *The Monkey's Wedding* from the war-torn town of Foçjau. The painting is now on its way to the National Gallery in London, where . . ."

Is it, though? thought Mrs. Invach, scowling, switching off the TV set. I'd like to see them get their hands on it before *I* come to a decision about it.

She ate her soup and conducted her evening search, more random than usual, but triumphantly unearthing a set of croquet mallets and an album full of Siberian stamps. Then she went to bed, after feeding the peregrines. But in the middle of the night they woke her, keening and mewing in the darkness of her bedroom.

"What is it, what's to do?" she demanded.

And was answered by a frantic cry from the floor, somewhere near her bed.

"Murder, *murder,* they're killing me, they're digging their claws into my *brain!* Make them get off, make them let go of me! Arrgh, you brutes, you monsters!"

Both birds had settled firmly onto the head of someone who had been crawling towards the bed from the doorway: beaks and talons were embedded in his scalp. Mrs. Invach observed the situation in the dim starlight from the huge windows, and smiled grimly.

"How did *you* get in? Oliver Twist? Eh?"

"Through the round window—they'll blind me—it's a torture—oh, please, please!"

"Have you accomplices outside?"

"Yes, in a truck, waiting till I'd pierced the gas capsule and let them in—"

"A gas capsule, huh? Where is that, then?"

It was in his limp hand, already broken. Mrs. Invach, without comment, smashed a window with the croquet mallet and switched on the vacuum cleaner to blow instead of suck.

Then she called the police art theft squad on the special radio line they had insisted on installing when she refused conventional protection.

"I have a truck full of thieves in my garden. Can you take them away?"

"What about *me?*" whimpered the defeated figure on the floor. "For pity's sake—make these monsters leave go of me."

"You be quiet," she said, "or I'll order them to peck your eyes out."

He fell silent.

Police arrived like lightning, swarming over the garden, seizing the truck and its occupants. But Mrs. Invach utterly refused to let them into the house.

"I have my own security system, thank you very much!" she snapped at the sergeant.

After they had gone with their captives, leaving four men on guard outside, Mrs. Invach returned to her bedroom and ordered the peregrines to let go of their prey. He struggled to his knees, very dejected, rubbing fingers gingerly through his rumpled red hair. His tartan cap had fallen off onto the mat.

"Well, Oliver Twist?" repeated Mrs. Invach sourly. "What have you got to say for yourself?"

He was the boy from McCustody Security.

"I—I thought it would be a good way to get into the house—see the pictures—that was why I got in touch with them—because I'm small—could get through the round hole—"

He gave her a defeated, hangdog look.

"I know who you are," said Mrs. Invach after a long, long pause. "You are Amalçja Kodan's son."

He nodded, then shook his head. "No, her grandson. Anatol."

"Where are they? Your mother? Your grandmother?"

"Dead. Both."

"Ah, so," she said. "So I was right in that, at least."

The boy stared at her uncomprehendingly. "My mother died five years ago. She said—she was always saying—that I should see my grandfather—get in touch—"

The old woman sniffed.

"Why should he want to see you? What use could *you* be to him?"

Anatol stiffened defensively. "I am a painter too!"

"Ha! You? At—how old are you?"

"Eighteen. And I have studied. And I know how to restore canvases—I am an expert—"

At eighteen? At eighteen, she thought, Jan was well under way.

But this boy?

"What I wanted—but what I really wanted," he said, "was to hear the tapes. All those tapes you have. I read about them in the paper. My grandfather, talking as he painted. Well, I wanted to meet him, of course. That was why—it took a long time to get to this country."

"It would not have been any use, your seeing him," she said. "He never talked to anybody. Not really. But the tapes—"

Drawing in a sharp breath, she switched on the player in her bedroom.

". . . Clouds like piano keys; shine of water in the shadow dark green and thick like sump oil—tree full of white eyes, each one looking a different way—hand sunk in the fur, very solid, reddish, artisan's hand, thick with bone—not at all like my hands, mine long and skinny, skeleton's hands very nearly—like the old girl's hands, hers on the way to skeleton, her face color of bleached mummy—now, touch of dark red here, stroke it on—yellow-green light moving towards saffron . . ."

She had switched on the light. She saw the boy had angry tears in his eyes.

"Why couldn't I meet him?"

"He's dead."

"I know. I heard on my transistor."

"But I have all the tapes here. And a lot of the pictures."

Mrs. Invach took stock of the boy, measuring him grimly. "Well, you can come here and listen to the tapes, I suppose. If you like."

His eyes blazed. "Yes! And can I see *The Monkey's Wedding?*"

"Very well."

She led the way downstairs to the dining room, where the picture still lay spread out on the massive old table. She switched on all the lights, and heard a policeman cough and stamp outside.

The boy began to walk slowly around the table, around

and around, stopping sometimes, with his face close to the surface, to peer at a crack, or a bullet hole, or a bloodstain, never quite touching the canvas, but his eyes almost stroking it, his hands making small, blind, fluttering movements, as if they held invisible tools.

Old Mrs. Invach, perched on a high stool, watched him.

As he walked round and round, back and forth, he began to mutter, to breathe out an inaudible monologue, to discuss with some unseen auditor how he would do this, would do that, how he would set about repairing the canvas . . .

After a while Mrs. Invach wandered away and left him to it, and began again her own endless search for lost things.

About Joan Aiken

Writing short stories has always been my favorite occupation ever since I was small, when I used to tell stories to my younger brother on walks we took through the Sussex woods and fields. At first I told him stories out of books we had in the house, and then, running low on these, I began to invent, using the standard ingredients: witches, dragons, castles. Then doors began to open in my mind; I realized that the stories could be enriched and improved by mixing in everyday situations—people catching trains, mending punctures in bicycle tires, winning raffles, getting medicine from the doctor.

Then I began mixing in dreams. I have always had wonderful dreams—not as good as those of my father, Conrad Aiken, who was the best dreamer I ever met, but very striking and full of mystery and excitement. The first story I ever finished, written at age six or seven, was taken straight from a dream. It was called "Her Husband Was a Demon." And one of my full-length books, *Midnight Is a Place* was triggered off by a formidable dream about a carpet factory. Most of my short stories have some connection with a dream. When I awake, I jot down the important element of the dream in a small notebook. Then weeks, months, even years may go by before I use it, but in the end a connection will be made with something that is happening *now,* and that sets off a story.

It is rather like mixing flour and yeast and warm water. All three ingredients, on their own, will stay unchanged, but put them together and fermentation begins. A short story is not planned, in the way that a full-length novel is planned, episode by episode, with the end in sight; a short story is *given,* straight out of nowhere: Suddenly two elements combine and the whole pattern is there, in the same way as, I imagine, painters get a vision of their pictures, before work starts. A short story, to me, always has a mysterious component, something that appears inexplicably from nowhere. Inexplicably, but inevitably; for if you check back through the pattern of the story, you can see that the groundwork has already been laid for it.

The Monkey's Wedding was set in motion by a dream about an acerbic old lady hunting about her house for lost things and buried memories, combined with a news story about a valuable painting found abandoned in a barn; only after I had begun the story did I realize that the last ingredient was going to be a grandson she didn't even know she had lost.

JOAN AIKEN is the author of about ninety books for adults and children, including novels, plays, one collection of verse, and many collections of short stories and ghost stories. She is the recipient of the Edgar Award for Best Juvenile Mystery from the Mystery Writers of America for her novel, *Nightfall*. Her latest book for children is *Cold Shoulder Road*. She lives in Petworth, Sussex, with her husband, Julius Goldstein, and they go back and forth to New York, where he comes from. She has two children, John and Lizza, and two grandchildren, Belou and Emil.

"*Where's your pa?*" *he rasped.*

"*In Saudi Arabia.*"

"*That's just great.*" *In the soft light of the porch, I could tell he was frightened. "I just killed a man on the beach.*"

THE GRIND OF AN AXE
BY THEODORE TAYLOR

The call from a girl who said she was Gudrid Karlsevne, from the island of Bornholm, off Sweden, came through about three thirty in the afternoon, California time. She said she was answering the ad in the Stockholm newspaper for a nurse-maid. She was the first of several girls named Karlsevne who answered it.

I knew that my father, Snorre Karlsevne, had placed such an ad. My mother was a career woman in stocks and bonds and intended to return to work after giving birth.

"Neither my mother or father are here," I said.

I told Gudrid, who spoke English with a soft accent and sounded very nice, that I was their daughter, Wendy, and would have my mother call her back. Mother was at the doctor's office, the baby due in a month. My father, who worked for Cal-Aero, was in Saudi Arabia, expected home within two weeks, in time for the estimated arrival of my new brother or sister.

"Have you ever been to America?" I asked.

"No, but I hope I can come over and take care of the new child."

I asked how old she was.

"Twenty."

Since I was sixteen, I thought it might be fun to be around her. She was probably tall, blond, and beautiful and could tell me all sorts of things about Scandinavia. I promised I'd have my mother call her back the minute she returned.

In the ad, my father had requested that the nursemaid be named Karlsevne. Let me explain: My father is a Vikingperson just like there are American Irishpersons and Britishpersons and Frenchpersons and Dutchpersons, who often make bores out of themselves talking about the *auld sod*, Trafalgar Square, Paris, and Rotterdam.

My father would proudly tell anyone that Torfinn Karlsevne was the first man to discover America, 488 years before Columbus. I once made the mistake of showing him an article that said Leif Ericsson reached either Newfoundland or Nova Scotia in A.D. 999. Either way, Norwegians discovered America.

Jaw set, blue eyes impaling me, he said, "Thorfinn, or Torfinn, and his wife had a son named Snorre, and that's eventually how I got my name. It all happened at Hudson Bay." Then he showed me a book that said the same thing. According to the family tree, my father was the seventy-eighth Snorre Karlsevne.

My mother, Harriet, got home from the doctor about twenty minutes later and I told her about the call from Bornholm. She laughed and shook her head. "Gudrid is the first name of your father's great-great grandmother. He'll be pleased. What a family!" She always tended to laugh about the Viking thing. She was a farm girl from Kansas and demanded good English names for her children. Hence, Wendy is my name.

She called Bornholm a few minutes later and talked with Gudrid for a long time, finally asking for her personal recommendations and phone numbers from people in Sweden who could speak English. We received a fax within an hour and within a few days she got the job. A date was set for her to arrive in San Francisco in two weeks.

After that conversation, a strange thing happened. Looking back, it all seemed so innocent but it brought us to the brink of terror. Operator 651, in San Francisco, called to say she had a cablegram from Sweden addressed to my father. The operator read it while Mother copied it down: "Delighted to know you exist. Thought I was the last Karlsevne on earth. Will arrive Friday night SAS at 11:40. Cousin Torfinn."

My mother sat with her mouth open. "This is crazy," she said. 'I'm about to have a baby; your father is in Saudi Arabia, and his cousin . . . " She stopped and blew out a deep breath. " . . . is coming here. He doesn't ask, doesn't leave a phone number . . ."

She sat a few minutes longer, then typically, tried to do something about the visitor. Stop him! She placed another call to Gudrid, and the female voice that answered spoke Swedish. "*Var så god,*" she said. "Please." Five minutes passed before a male voice said, over thousands of miles, that Gudrid had taken the ferry to the mainland to ski for a week before going to America. The voice was heavily accented.

"Do you know Torfinn Karlsevne?" my mother asked.

I'd gone upstairs to listen on the other phone.

'I've heard of him," the man said warily, as if he didn't want to discuss Torfinn Karlsevne. That was puzzling.

"Does he have a phone number?"

There was a moment's pause, as if a family decision was being made. "No."

My mother thanked him and hung up. I went back downstairs. She was still by the phone. Angry now. "Wouldn't you know your father would be away when this happens."

As she proceeded to dial Riyadh, the capital of Saudi, I went back upstairs to listen and say hi to my dad. There was a time lapse of eleven hours between the California coast and

Riyadh, so it would be about five A.M., Thursday, where he was.

Awakened from a deep sleep, he sounded groggy, but my mother ignored that state to tell him she didn't appreciate his unknown cousin's visit; that he better find some way to get in touch with his cousin and make him delay his trip until after the baby was born. *Well* after!

I broke in to say, "Hi, Pop . . . "

"How yuh doin', Wendy?"

I said I was fine and looked forward to meeting Gudrid.

My mother and father talked for almost a half hour. Argued. Finally, he said, "Let him stay for two or three days, then tell him he has to go."

"Snorre, you don't know this man. He could be a thief, an addict, a rapist . . ."

"If his name is Karlsevne, he's a good man, Harriet. I've never heard anything bad about a Karlsevne . . ."

"Oh?" Her voice was full of gravel. "Well, that's reassuring. He's going to sleep here even if he might be a rapist. I'm going to cook for him. Should I make *frikadeller?* How about *hakkebiff?* How about me buying a bottle of *Taffel Akvavit?*" Akvavit was Scandinavian liquor.

"Come on, Harriet . . ."

My mother didn't say her usual "I love you" before hanging up.

Our old house, less than a hundred yards from the crashing California surf, had a New England smack about it, a stately Maine solidity. It fitted in rather perfectly with the other vintage cottages, mostly weathered shingle.

All told, there were only five houses on that secluded stretch of Avesta Beach. It was sometimes dark and lonely during the gray fall and winter months. But my father liked it that way, though my mother didn't. Born in Minnesota, his

Scandinavian blood demanded a slice of the old country coast. Avesta Beach, with its guano-whitened rocks and leisurely beds of kelp, often had the misty moods of *fjords*. It was, truly, a place for Vikings.

About six-thirty two nights later, there was a heavy rap on the front door. Visitors were few after sundown, and I looked at my mother and she looked back at me, frowning at the door, eyes narrowing.

"See who it is, Wendy," she said. Our visitor was not due until the following morning. It takes a while to get from San Francisco to Avesta.

I opened the door, and standing there was a man of about fifty, I estimated. He had a robust red beard. He was a huge man, dressed in a blue flannel shirt, brown corduroy pants of European cut, red kerchief around his thick neck. A black leather jacket encased his big shoulders. His hair was red-brown, curling around his ears. Cousin Torfinn, of course, eyes of Baltic blue.

The big man grinned broadly, looking around and behind us. My mother had joined me. "Where is Cousin Snorre?"

"In Saudi Arabia," my mother said bleakly.

"What's he doing there?"

Torfinn spoke with the slightest chamois rub of Norselander.

"He's a missile defense expert. How did you get here? Your plane isn't due until 11:40 tonight."

"It was early. I took a bus."

My mother nodded, but I saw suspicion as she glanced at me. The only bus going near Avesta passed at about three-thirty P.M. daily. "I'm Harriet, and this is our daughter, Wendy."

Torfinn said quaintly, and with great charm, "You're a beautiful woman and with child."

Mother laughed nervously. "Yes, with child."

"How soon?"

"Three weeks or so."

"It will be a boy, a strong boy, a handsome boy," Cousin Torfinn said confidently.

"Perhaps," Mother said, allowing a smile. I could see that she was beginning to succumb to the winter-sky-blue eyes and the ivory grin of my father's cousin. Torfinn was at least six feet four and had the most powerful hands I'd ever seen.

Mother said, "Well, take off your coat and Wendy will show you to your room." His belongings were in an old canvas seabag.

Downstairs again, I went into the kitchen. Mother was by the stove. We were having soup that night. There was no problem in setting another bowl.

"Check SAS for me," she said, stirring the soup. She was still a little suspicious.

Just then, Torfinn clumped down the stairs and we walked back into the living room. He went to the beach-facing window. "I knew you'd live by the sea. It's in Snorre's blood. He'll sail eternally. Viking blood he's got. The tide goes in and out of his body."

"I suppose so," my mother said. "I'll put dinner on."

I said, "Let me show you something, Cousin Torfinn." I steered him into my father's library-home office. There were shelves of Viking books, models of long-ships; Viking shields and swords.

"It was a great age," he said approvingly. "History has never given us Vikings our just place." *Our!*

There was an old map on one wall. He said, "At one time we had Iceland, the Faroe, Norway, Sweden, Denmark, England, France, Holland, Scotland . . ."

He tapped a big finger at Gairsey, near the Pentland Firth,

on the Scottish coast. "Sweyn Asliefssen used to come here. In the summer evenings you could hear the grind of swords and axes over ten hills and valleys."

I noticed Mother in the doorway, listening; amused.

During dinner, Torfinn talked about Thor, Ottar, and Leif Ericsson. About Halfdan Longlegs and Ragnar Hairybreeks and Harald Bluetooth. Told stories about them. "Ah, they were mighty men."

He was wonderful, and I knew Dad would love to hear him. How could I hang on to his cousin for another ten days?

"My father was Magnus Karlscvne and he traced our immediate family back to A.D. 605."

My mother murmured, "That's a long time back."

Torfinn nodded. "Now, the baby. You'll name him Snorre, of course."

"I doubt that very much. I prefer Michael or Mark," she answered crisply.

Frowning, he said, "Shame!" Then he repeated angrily, "Shame!"

My mother remained silent.

"You *will* name him Snorre!" His eyes were fierce.

My mother said, calmly, "We will name him what we choose to name him, or her, Cousin Torfinn."

The big man glared at her and finished his meal in silence, then said, "I'd like to take a walk. Do you mind?"

"Not at all," Mother said.

As soon as the door closed, none too gently, behind him, Mother said to me, "Call SAS. I want to know exactly when he arrived."

I did as told. The lady at SAS said, "Sorry, no passenger by that name on last night's flight."

I went back to the kitchen and lied. "He came in last night." I didn't want to see him kicked out before Dad came home. I believed that my mother would warm to Cousin Torfinn in a day or two. But I also wondered how he'd gotten here so quickly. He didn't look like a man who'd take a taxi all the way from San Francisco.

We went up to bed, and I think Mother fell asleep right away. With the baby banging around inside her, she caught sleep when she could.

I stayed awake, thinking about our visitor, and SAS and my lie, and then over the moaning wind I heard a voice. I got up and went to the window. Mr. Kelly, our next-door neighbor, was below. He shouted again. "Snorre, I've got to talk to you . . ."

"Daddy isn't here. I'll come down." I slipped on a robe.

Old Kelly was on the porch with a rifle in his hands. A small, wizened man of about seventy, he had large bloodshot eyes and skin the color of tallow. He was half deaf and couldn't see very well.

"Where's your pa?" he rasped.

"In Saudi Arabia."

"That's just great." In the soft light of the porch, I could tell he was frightened. "I just killed a man on the beach."

"You did *what?*" I could barely speak.

"I saw a man go by my place, a stranger. You know I don't like strangers. So I got my gun and followed him. I found him up by the rocks grinding an axe against them. I yelled at him, but he paid no attention. Then all of a sudden he turned and I saw the blade of the axe . . ."

Mr. Kelly stopped and took a deep breath. "I fired."

"Oh, my God," I said. "What did he look like?"

"A big, ugly brute with a red beard."

My heart slammed. "Stay here, Mr. Kelly. I'll get dressed."

I quickly pulled on jeans, a sweatshirt, and tennies and took off, grabbing a flashlight. *Cousin Torfinn shot?*

With Mr. Kelly I hurried over the sand toward the outcropping about a quarter mile north, heart thumping, mouth dry.

We go to the rocks and Mr. Kelly said, "Shine it over there." There was no body draining blood.

"Well, I'll be double-damned. He's not here."

"Are you sure you shot him? Did you see him fall?"

Mr. Kelly laughed sourly. "No, I panicked, Wendy. I ran! What did you expect me to do? But I tell you I shot a prowler out here twenty minutes ago. I'm old, but not crazy."

I looked around and shouted, "Torfinn! Cousin Torfinn!"

The only answer was the crash of surf; the moan of the damp salted wind.

"Who are you calling?" Mr. Kelly asked.

"My dad's cousin. He arrived here tonight from Sweden."

"Big fellow with a beard?"

"Yes."

Mr. Kelly suddenly became enraged. "What the devil was he doing with an axe?"

"I don't know," I answered weakly. My knees felt like melting butter. "But I'll try to find out. I'm glad you missed him."

Mr. Kelly grumbled, "Yeah. Tell him he got lucky."

A glazed half-moon was lodged in the sky, high over the fog bank that lay offshore. Faintly, over the south-blowing breeze, I could hear a joyful singsong baritone:

And then there was Torfinn
Who dealt a mighty blow
And chopped off the head of
The Merry Earl of Stoe . . .

I shivered, thankful Mr. Kelly couldn't hear it, and said to him, "We might as well go home."

"My rheumatism agrees."

We walked back to the five houses and I said good night to old Kelly.

"Tell him to stay off the beach at night if he wants to live," he advised.

"I will," I said. Then I added, "Please don't say anything to my mother about this. With the baby due, she's already nervous."

"All right," he grumbled and went on into his house.

I went into our house and into my father's "Viking" room and took Sorenson's *Viking Years,* the most accurate of all his reference books, off the shelf. I read: ". . . after killing Thangbrand and Thorvald, Thorfinn's last conquest before setting sail for Hudson Bay was the beheading of the Earl of Stoe. It is a matter of record that he killed eleven men, but records of that period are conservative and one may safely count at least twenty heads that fell victim to Thorfinn's wrath with his sword and axe."

I sat there a while thinking about Cousin Torfinn. He certainly wasn't a ghost. I could stick my finger in his chest and it would hit flesh. But that fiendish song bothered me.

In bed again, I tossed and turned, waiting to hear Torfinn's heavy feet on the stairs. But I finally fell asleep, thinking about the "body" Mr. Kelly thought he saw; thinking about my SAS lie.

In the morning, Torfinn was already in the kitchen when I went downstairs. Coffee was on. He'd made himself at home. I said, "You see anyone on the beach last night during your walk?"

"Not a soul. I owned the sand and stars. It was glorious."

"Our neighbor said he saw a man grinding an axe up by the rocks. He said the man was big and had a beard."

Torfinn smiled. "Hmmmmmm . . . " The smile said more than words.

I said, innocently, "I still can't figure out how you got here so early yesterday when your plane wasn't due until almost midnight."

He kept smiling. "Oh, I cabled you the wrong date. I arrived night before last, slept at the airport, took a bus south yesterday; then walked in from the highway . . ."

That all seemed to check out, even though SAS said he wasn't listed. But airlines do make mistakes. And it would have taken him three hours to walk in from 101. I almost felt ashamed at having doubted him. Actually, it was my mother who was suspicious.

Just then she waddled in. "Good morning."

Torfinn grinned back. "*God morgon.*"

"Did you have a nice walk last night?" she asked.

"Ah, it was glorious. The tide was beginning to rush the way it does in The Skaw."

"I'm glad," she said and went about fixing breakfast. She seemed rested and relaxed.

I went out to get the newspaper and saw our axe by the corner of the garage. It was freshly sharpened and polished. *So he was by the rocks last night!* Old Kelly had missed.

When I went inside, Torfinn was on the phone talking to my father in Swedish. Now and then Torfinn would laugh heartily. They were having a good time. Mother and I felt out of it. I helped her with the dishes, wondering about Kelly and his rifle. Goofy old man.

Finally, Torfinn got off the phone and handed it to my mother. Immediately, she said, "I'll take it upstairs."

Torfinn nodded and said, "I have a job to do outside."

What job? I had my own to do, straightening my room, always a weekend chore.

Soon, Mother came in. She said, angrily, "Your father didn't ask his cousin to leave. He'll come home next Saturday. Meanwhile, he said if I wanted Torfinn to go, just ask him.

He hoped I wouldn't." She sighed deeply and sat down on the edge of my bed. "It's just bad timing." Then she grunted. The baby had drop-kicked her.

About an hour later, I went downstairs and then out to the backyard. Wood chips were flying from the axe blade. I asked Torfinn what he was doing.

"Building a cradle for Snorre, the seventy-ninth."

Dad's hobby was woodworking. He had power tools and wood in a shed behind the garage. Torfinn had taken some white pine from the bin. "This cradle will not have a single piece of iron in it. I'll put it together with pegs, the way Vikings did theirs."

I called Mother out of the house to view the handiwork. She looked at it and said, "Torfinn, I received a beautiful bassinet at a shower two weeks ago. The baby will sleep in it."

He looked hurt, even angry, again. "You wait! This will be the most beautiful cradle you've ever seen."

She nodded, rolled her eyes, and returned inside.

I stayed out there awhile and watched him work, asking about Harald Bluetooth and Ragnar Hairybreeks and Kalf Scurvy and Jon Limpleg and Thorir Treebeard.

He finished the cradle in late afternoon and came into the house to say, "Now we must dedicate it."

Returning outside, my mother was impressed. "It's exquisite. You did all that with an axe?"

"Of course," he answered. "Now, I will take it to the sea and dip it. You will witness."

We looked at the towering redheaded man. His hands were like giant clamshells. Mother agreed meekly.

Soon, we stood at water's edge, where foam lay in sudsy coils. Torfinn waded in over his boots and gently placed the *krubba* in the sea, talking to it, first in Swedish, then in English: "The sea will swell your seams and fill you with strength; the child that rests within your arms will someday return to The Skaw and Pentland Firth . . ."

My mother had tears in her eyes at the simple unforgettable charm of the ceremony.

I discovered Mr. Kelly's body halfway between the house and the rocks. I'd gone to his house to tell him that Cousin Torfinn was a very nice man. After all, he'd built a cradle for the baby. Mr. Kelly wasn't home, and I went out looking for him. He often surf-fished in late afternoon.

About two hours after his body was taken off to the mortuary, I sat in the front room with my mother and a uniformed officer. He'd already talked briefly to Cousin Torfinn. Finally, the office said, "An autopsy will tell us what happened." We'd told him about Mr. Kelly's heart condition.

"He was a wonderful old man," my mother said. "We'll miss him."

After the officer departed, I went out to the tool room where Torfinn was painting flower designs on the head and sides of the cradle. I said, "Did you see our neighbor on the beach today?"

"Yes."

"Did you talk to him today?"

Torfinn nodded.

"How did he look?"

"He looked very ill the last time I saw him."

After dinner I went to the front porch where Torfinn was sitting. He looked over and said, poetically, "The waves are fighting each other tonight. There's a storm somewhere, far off. In the other ocean I could tell you where. Maybe off the Faroe, or as far away as the Azores. I can tell by the sound of the sea, and the taste of the wind."

Maybe he was a real Viking, a ghost of the man who discovered America. Maybe he was both living and dead.

Sitting beside him I watched the surf for a long time, the long white lines advancing in the darkness, then I said, "Cousin Torfinn, what happened to Harry Kelly today?"

He deliberated a moment, then said, "You are family and dear to me. I would not lie to you. He died of fright."

Horrified, I asked, "You frightened him to death?"

He laughed curiously. "Me? Heaven forbid. No, no. If it happened, it was accidental."

"What did happen?"

"I was half asleep in the sun on the beach, with my eyes closed, and I heard someone coming. I felt them bending over. I could feel breath in my face. I suddenly opened my eyes and shouted, 'Boo.' The poor man keeled over."

"Why didn't you tell us? Why did you leave him there? Why didn't you tell the officer when he questioned you?"

He frowned at me in amazement. "I'm a visitor here. I'm an alien. It would not go well."

Mr. Kelly was dead, and he was responsible. Yet it didn't bother him. I said, "You must leave. It isn't working out the way I planned. Now, we have to tell the police."

"What good would that do? Do you try a man in court for saying 'Boo'?"

"I have to tell my mother," I said.

He said, slowly, but with determination, "Your brother must be Snorre. You must order your mother to do that. And I must be the godfather. After he is born and christened, I will go. I did not mean to cause you trouble."

In despair, I said, "This isn't the old country, Cousin Torfinn. No one can order my mother to do anything."

The bearded man looked off at the white hilltops of sea. "Then I will stay longer and deal with your father," he said flatly. It sounded like a threat.

So that I wouldn't upset my mother, I decided to wait until Dad returned Saturday to tell him about everything that had happened. Then he could deal with it.

But something else had happened. Mother had changed her mind about Cousin Torfinn. She said to me, "I guess I'm just a nutty female 'with child,' as he said." She admitted she was beginning to understand how he felt about having a family name for the newborn. She would now agree to Snorre, Jr.

I stood there openmouthed. She'd argued with my father over my name. He'd wanted Piger or Jenter or Flickor and she'd absolutely refused. Now, she was going to accept Snorre, Jr. Cousin Torfinn had bewitched her. I couldn't believe it.

I said, "Are you sure?"

She nodded, almost teary-eyed. I guess pregnant women become emotional in their last weeks.

The next day when Torfinn was out of the house, I did a sneaky thing. I looked around his room. There was a half-empty bottle of *akvavit* and he'd taken one of Dad's broadswords. I guess he was polishing it, maybe sharpening it. Steel wool and linseed oil were beside it on the table. The blade gleamed.

Late that same evening, while he was on another of his long beach walks, there was a rap on the front door. I opened it and a tall girl stood there. A Yellow Cab from Watsonville was at the end of our walk. The girl was not beautiful. She was quite plain. Oddly enough, on her face was fright.

Her first words were, "My name is Gudrid Karlsevne. I'm from Bornholm . . ."

I started to say, "Welcome," but her second words spilled out.

"Is my Uncle Torfinn here?"

"Yes," I said. "He's walking the beach."

"Do you have an axe?" Her eyes were wide.

"Yes."

"Where is it?"

"By the woodpile."

"Is it there now?"

"It was this afternoon."

"Look now."

We hurried to the rear of the garage. No axe.

Then words rushed out. Face chalky white, blue eyes big, hands trembling. Gudrid said, "He's insane. He escaped from Bornholm Hospital the evening after I visited him and told him I was coming to America to Cousin Snorre Karlsevne's house in California to be a nursemaid. I told him everything, without thinking. After he escaped, he went to his house, and got his passport, got money he'd hidden before the murder trial. None of my family ever thought he'd come here. They thought he'd gone to Norway or Denmark. So did I. But then on the plane coming here, I thought, 'Could he have gone to your house?' I'm so sorry. He's very clever. He has that terrible disease, one minute kind and gentle; the next he'll kill you if you make him angry . . ."

As she was saying all of that, the cold edge of the wind carried a singsong baritone:

And then there was Torfinn
Who dealt a mighty blow
And chopped off the head of
The Merry Earl of Stoe . . .

I ran to call 911.

About Theodore Taylor

What fun, what enjoyment, it is to read and write detective/mystery/suspense novels and short stories. I'm usually escorted into sleep each night with Sue Grafton or Mary Higgins Clark or Elmore Leonard, or a dozen other fine practitioners.

As a writer, I do a mixed bag—war, action-adventure, suspense/mystery, even a historical now and then, both for young adults and adults. I enjoy switching back and forth. Long ago, I wrote a number of short stories for men's magazines (*Stag, Male, Argosy,* etc.) and I'm so glad that Lois Duncan invited me to try again.

I was lucky enough to win the Mystery Writers of America Award for Best Young Adult category in 1991 with *The Weirdo,* set in a brooding North Carolina swamp. Add a dead body, a missing body, some black bears, a sand suck and a boy with burn scars on his face and you have the proper ingredients.

The Grind of an Axe dates back to working on a film in Denmark and Sweden in 1959. I got involved in Viking lore and brought home a number of nonfiction books on the subject. The Vikings were larger than life, of course, and I became fascinated with these hearty, sword-swinging men.

I began writing at the age of thirteen for a daily newspaper and have been pecking away on an upright manual typewriter for more than sixty years: five newspapers, novels, nonfiction, magazines, radio, television, motion pictures. It's been a wonderful, rewarding word-trip.

She tore at the coils, but they did not budge. Panic flooded through her like a riptide. "Mel, it won't come off!"

Mel jumped forward and yanked at the serpent's tail. The bracelet clung to Christy's arm as if it had grown into her skin. Her body prickled with the sting of a thousand ants . . .

"Mel, I can't stand it! I want it off, I want it off NOW!"

THE CHOSEN

BY MADGE HARRAH

Christy's first thought when she tried on the bracelet: *How weird.*

Her second thought: *I have to have it.*

The snake, a flexible band of golden metal, wrapped three times around the lower half of her right arm. The cobra-shaped head, which nestled near her wrist, surveyed the world with glittering ruby eyes.

"Hey, Mel, what do you think?" she asked, holding out her arm.

Melanie glanced up from the earring tray. Her freckled face creased in a frown when she saw the bracelet.

"Gross! You're not gonna buy that, are you?"

Christy shrugged. "Okay, so you hate snakes. I think it's cool."

The swarthy woman behind the flea market table grinned and nodded. Her earrings, clusters of foreign-looking coins, jangled discordantly.

"Only five dollars," she said.

Christy peeled the bracelet from her wrist and turned to examine it more closely in the sunlight. Surprise zinged down her spine when she saw the tiny letters stamped inside the band: 14K. But it couldn't be gold, not for only five dollars.

Or could it?

Maybe the woman didn't realize how much the bracelet was really worth.

"I'll take it," Christy said quickly, not wanting the woman to change her mind. "Can I just go ahead and wear it?"

"But of course you must wear it."

The woman's husky voice carried an accent that sounded familiar. Greek, Christy decided. Her grandfather had come from Greece and had told her many stories about the islands there.

"Yes, you must wear it," the woman repeated. "You have been chosen. It is meant to be."

Weird, Christy thought again.

But she had to have the bracelet. She once more wrapped the snake around her wrist, then pulled a five-dollar bill from her pocket. The woman took the money and handed her a card in exchange.

"I'm only out here at the flea market on Saturdays," the woman said. "Here is the address of my actual shop in case you need—" She fixed her eyes on Christy with a look so piercing that for a moment the impact made Christy dizzy. "In case you need any more unusual jewelry."

Christy got the feeling the woman had started to finish the sentence in some other way. She glanced at the card the woman had handed her:

SERVANT OF THE GODDESS
Antiques, old jewelry, collectibles
Claudia Popadopalus

The address and phone number were also printed on the card, along with a photograph of a small statuette, cracked and chipped as if it were very old. The figure was that of a young woman, slender, naked to the waist, with a snake wrapped around each arm. The legend beneath the picture read: Snake Goddess, Crete, 1500 B.C.

Crete. An island off the Greek coast, Christy remembered. Her grandfather had called it an island of mystery where young people had been sacrificed to strange gods thousands of years ago.

She slipped the card into her pocket, then grabbed Melanie's arm and pulled her away, hurrying down the line of tables and booths before the woman could call them back.

"Hey, what's the rush?" Mel protested.

Only when they had edged through the crowd to the next line of booths did Christy pause. "This bracelet—it's real gold. I don't want her to ask for it back."

"You paid for it. It's yours." Mel grimaced, wrinkling her nose. "Though why you want it, I don't know."

Christy held out her arm again. "Don't you like it at all?"

"No, it gives me the creeps."

"One garter snake in your bed when you were little and now you've got this phobia." Christy laughed at the memory.

Melanie threw her a hurt look. "What about you and fire? I'm not the only one with a phobia."

Fire.

Christy shuddered. A cracking sound filled her ears, the pungent smell of smoke seared her nostrils. She had been only five when her tree house had caught on fire, ignited by the candle she had lit despite her parents' orders not to play with matches. Now, nine years later, she still lived in horror of being trapped again by fire as she had been trapped that day in the tree. She had climbed higher and higher to avoid the licking flames until she reached the limber branches at the top, which had bent under her weight, lowering her once more toward the blaze, Her terrified screams had brought her father running with the hose—

"Mel, you're right. I'm sorry."

Mel socked her arm. "No problem. Listen, I'm getting

hungry, how about you? My mom gave me some extra money so we could buy a pizza for supper."

"My mom gave me extra money, too." Christy shook her head with wonder. "When my parents said they were going out of town for the weekend with your parents, I thought they'd make us stay with—"

"A sitter?" Mel groaned and made a face.

"Well, at least they finally admitted we're old enough to stay by ourselves," Christy said. "I just wish we were old enough to drive. Think what we could do this weekend if we had a car!"

Mel sighed and rolled her eyes. "Don't even mention it."

"Tell you what, let's buy ice cream, too, and rent a bunch of movies and stay awake all night."

"Let's do it."

Mel held out her hand with the little finger bent, and Christy hooked her own finger around it in their special sign that had meant "best friends" since kindergarten. During all these years, nothing had ever come between them for very long, not even their fights. Like the argument over this bracelet. Just a temporary thing, no big deal.

But try as she would that night, Christy could not stay awake. Even with all the lights on in her room and the television blaring, she felt her eyelids droop as if they were being pulled down by strings.

Mel, stretched out on the other bed, stifled a yawn. "This is weird. It's only midnight and I can't keep my eyes open."

"I can't, either. Hey, let's turn off the lights and make up ghost stories like we did when we were little. You go first."

"Okay."

With the room in darkness except for the greenish glow cast by her bedside digital clock, Christy settled back against her pillow while Mel's voice murmured in sepulchral tones,

"Once upon a time in an old house in the country there lived a madman who liked to chop up his neighbors for dinner . . ."

Christina, whispered a voice in Christy's ear. "*Come, Christina, come.*

The whispers blended with Mel's droning voice, washing over Christy in a hypnotic flow.

". . . and so the old man said to the girl—"

Come, Christina.

"He opened the door and motioned her inside—"

Come, come.

"Christy!" Mel's whisper hissed with fear.

Come.

"Christy, wake up!"

Christy opened her eyes and stared, confused, into the green-tinged gloom. She felt strangely lethargic, as if she had swallowed a sleeping pill. Half caught in a dream, she dimly realized that her right arm ached. Perhaps she had sprained her wrist, she thought, and someone had wound the stretch bandage too tight.

Then the bandage moved. Slowly, sinuously, it slithered along her arm. A tongue, feather-light, brushed her skin.

She was already off the bed and on her feet by the time Mel cried, "No, don't move!"

Before her stood a girl, dead-white, her dark hair braided around her head. A long white skirt banded with gold covered the lower part of the girl's body, but her breasts were bare. Golden vipers encircled the girl's arms, vipers that lifted their heads and hissed, revealing dripping fangs.

The Snake Goddess.

Christy looked into the goddess' glowing evil eyes.

And realized, with a surge of horror, that she was looking into her own eyes in a mirror.

Fire flared behind her, torches held by many hands. She

felt the heat pound against her flesh, heard the snap of flaming wood. She closed her eyes and swayed on a tree branch that dipped closer and closer toward the crackling blaze—

"Christy!"

Mel's voice, frantic with fear, sliced the air. Christy opened her eyes, blinking against the sudden brightness in the room. The other girl had vanished from the mirror. Christy viewed her own image, dark hair tousled, shorts and T-shirt wrinkled, snake bracelet back in place. She whirled to see Mel pressed against the wall, her hand on the light switch, her eyes wide with terror.

"That girl . . . that girl with the snakes," Mel stammered.

"You saw her, too?"

"I thought for a minute she was you. What is it, what's happening?"

"I don't know. But I'm getting rid of this bracelet right now." She tore at the coils, but they did not budge. Panic flooded right through her like a riptide. "Mel, it won't come off!"

Mel jumped forward and yanked at the serpent's tail. The bracelet clung to Christy's arm as if it had grown into her skin. Her body prickled with the sting of a thousand ants. Bile burned her throat.

"Mel, I can't stand it! I want it off, I want it off NOW!" She fished the woman's card from her pocket and headed for the phone.

"She won't be at the store this late," Mel protested.

"Maybe she will. She sold this bracelet to me, she'd better know how to get it off."

To Christy's surprise, the woman answered the phone after only one ring.

"I'm the girl who—" she began.

"Who bought the bracelet today," the woman interrupted.

"Are you calling about the key?"

"What key?"

"The one that unlocks the bracelet. You dashed off this afternoon without it."

"I didn't know the bracelet locks."

"Sometimes it does, sometimes it doesn't."

"Look, something weird just happened . . . " Christy paused, suddenly realizing how crazy the story would sound. If she tried to explain, the woman might think she was on drugs. "The bracelet is giving me a rash, and I have to get it off," she amended.

"I'm sorry about the rash," the woman said. "Do you want to come now?"

Would that be possible? Christy wondered. She studied the address, but did not recognize the street. If it were not too far, perhaps she and Mel could ride their bikes.

"If that would be okay. I know it's late—"

"But of course you must come."

Come, Christina, come. The call tugged at her mind, her heart, filling her with a sweet lasstitude. She wanted to sink into that voice, lose herself in that voice . . . She shook her head, wondering if she were losing her mind.

"My shop is built onto the front of my house, and I often stay up until two or three in the morning," the woman went on. "Tell me where you are and I'll tell you how to get here."

As the woman dictated directions, Christy wrote them down on the cover of her phone book. Her heart sank when she realized the woman's house was over five miles away.

"Good-bye, Christina," the woman finished. "I'll be watching for you."

The dial tone sang in Christy's ear. She chilled, suddenly realizing that the woman had called her by name. Had Mel spoken her name in front of the woman that afternoon? She couldn't remember.

Aloud she said, "Mel, we'll have to take a cab. You got any money left?"

"Some. How about you?"

"Some. Let's hope it's enough."

Thirty minutes later the cab driver let them off in front of the antique shop, which had a sign above the door reading SERVANT OF THE GODDESS. The shop was attached to an old Victorian house that loomed over it like a bird of prey. Christy shivered when she noticed the street looked completely deserted.

"Are you girls gonna be okay?" the driver asked, sounding concerned.

Just then the shop door opened and the woman from the flea market stepped out onto the sidewalk. She smiled and lifted one hand in welcome.

"Yes, we'll be fine," Christy said quickly. Was it her imagination or had the bracelet moved again? "See, she's expecting us."

Only after the man had driven away did Christy realize she should have asked him to wait. For one brief moment she wished they hadn't come.

The bracelet suddenly tightened as if it had shrunk. Panic fluttered inside Christy's chest like an injured bird. What would happen if the bracelet drew so tight that it cut off the circulation to her hand? Yes, she had to have that key. But just as soon as the bracelet was off, she told herself, she and Mel would call another cab and get out of there.

"I'm so sorry you've had all this trouble," the woman said solicitously, urging them forward. "Come, girls, come, and we'll get that pesky old bracelet right off."

Come, Christina, come.

The whisper brushed past Christy's ear, softer than a sigh.

She listened for the whisper to repeat, but heard only the moan of the night wind.

"We'll just walk through the store into the house," the woman said as she ushered them inside.

Christy felt Mel's little finger curl around her own and knew she was uneasy, too.

"Please excuse the mess," the woman chattered on, "but I've got so much stuff, it's hard to keep it all dusted."

She led the way past piles of old furniture, display cases stacked with boxes, mannequins draped with hats and capes. One of the mannequins, half hidden in shadow, seemed to have the body of a person and the head of an animal. A buffalo? A bull?

"Here's the door that leads into my living quarters," the woman continued. "I've brewed a pot of tea so we can sit and have a little chat. Just call me Claudia, okay?"

She opened the door and motioned them through. Christy stepped into the room beyond, then paused, shocked by the sight of black-robed figures with flaming torches in their hands. But it was their heads, their huge, horned, shaggy heads, that turned her knees to pudding.

On the island of Crete, she now remembered, had once lived a monster called the Minotaur, a creature half-man and half-bull that craved human sacrifice.

She whirled just as Claudia slammed the door and slid a bolt into place.

Turning with a look of triumph on her face, Claudia announced in ringing tones, "Goddess, they are here."

"Chris," Mel wailed, "it's her!"

Christy whipped around once more, her heart pounding, her mouth dry. The room loomed ahead of her, impossibly long and tall, as if the house outside were but a shell to conceal some kind of temple. The Snake Goddess stood on a dais at the far end of the room, guarded on either side by smoking braziers. Her red eyes glowed, the serpents on her arm writhed and hissed. The snake on Christy's arm stirred and slithered one coil forward. Its wedge-shaped head lifted into the air.

Come, Christina, come, said the goddess without opening her mouth.

Christy heard the words inside her brain, felt them tug at her arms and legs. She stumbled several steps forward.

Come, Christina.

The voice inside Christy's head soothed and caressed, the hypnotic eyes burned into her own. She staggered closer still, pulled by invisible ropes.

"Goddess, we have brought the sacrifice," said Claudia.

"Christy, wh—what's happening?" Mel stammered.

Feeling as if she had no will of her own, Christy slowly turned her head to see Mel struggling nearby, her arms pinioned from behind by Claudia, whose hands looked as knotted and strong as a man's.

"Apply the snake, Christina," Claudia commanded. "The blood of the islands runs in your veins. You are the chosen one, the servant of the goddess. Apply the snake."

Apply the snake. The silent command of the goddess bored into Christy's brain.

Voices on either side of the room began a rhythmic chant. "Venom and flame, venom and flame, we worship you with venom and flame."

What did they want? Christy wondered. Dazed, she pivoted in a circle, trying to focus on the black-robed figures, the tapestries behind them that shifted as if stirred by wind, the diaphanous skirt of the goddess.

And then she knew. They wanted her to let the snake bite Mel.

The snake hissed and slithered forward one more coil, arching toward Mel's chest.

Apply the snake, commanded the goddess.

The insistent voice throbbed inside Christy's head. She slowly pushed one foot toward Mel.

"Apply the snake," said Claudia.

Another step.

"Chris, stop! Oh, please, please stop!" begged Mel, her face twisted with terror.

Christy paused, struggling against the alien force that burned inside her. What was she doing? This was Mel, her best friend, her friend who feared snakes above all else.

"Venom and flame," chanted the voices.

No. A tiny cry of defiance echoed from deep within Christy's consciousness.

"Apply the snake," insisted Claudia.

No, cried Christy's inner voice, growing stronger.

Apply the snake, commanded the goddess.

"No!" shouted Christy.

She leaped to one side and wrested the torch from the hand of the nearest black-robed monster. She clenched her teeth against the nausea that flooded her throat as she forced her wrist through the flame. The snake uncoiled like a released spring and fell writhing to the floor where it slithered beneath the hem of the monster's robe. The monster roared and jumped back, shaking his robe with both hands. Then, to Christy's astonishment, the monster's head fell off and rolled across the floor. Where she had previously looked into the fearful visage of a bull, she now saw the thin face of a man.

A man who had been wearing a mask.

"You're just a bunch of sick people playing a dumb game!" she shouted. Pointing toward Mel, she demanded, "Let her go, Claudia. Let her go."

When the robed figures started forward, Claudia called in commanding tones, "Let me handle this." Fixing her dark eyes on Christy, she said, "You are the servant of the goddess."

"Christina, you are mine," whispered the goddess.

Christy wavered, feeling again the lassitude, the sweet surrender, that had possessed her earlier. She concentrated on the pain in her burned wrist to force the feeling away.

"No. Let her go."

"You chose," insisted Claudia, her eyes fierce and compelling. "When you put on the bracelet, *you* chose. Now you belong to the goddess. You must obey her commands."

"You are mine," repeated the goddess.

Once more Christy focused on the pain in her wrist as she struggled against the magnetic pull of the voices. Strength swelled within her like a flower bursting into bloom.

"No! The gods of Crete died long ago. My grandfather told me so, and I believe him. See?" She ran the torch along the goddess's arm. "Wood. Maybe you're telepathic and maybe you're also a hypnotist, Claudia, I don't know. But I do know the voice of the goddess is yours."

Claudia let go of Mel's arm and leaped toward Christy, yelling, "Seize her!"

As the robed figures surged forward, Christy jumped onto the dais and found that Mel had joined her.

Dropping the torch, Christy yelled "Push!"

Together they toppled the statue toward the advancing horse. The statue's skirt billowed over the torch and burst into flame. Several of the robed figures, dodging away from the statue, fell against the tapestry. Their torches swept across pictures of birds, lilies, snakes, bulls, the maze of a labyrinth. Rivers of fire flowed through the cloth.

"Save the goddess!" shouted Claudia. "Don't let her burn."

The acrid smell of smoke seared Christy's nostrils, a crackling roar filled her ears. Trapped. Trapped by fire in a locked room. She swayed and would have fallen had Mel not grabbed her and punched her hard on the arm.

"Come on," Mel shouted. "We've got to get out of here!"

Restored by the blow, Christy leaped with Mel to one side, away from the scramble of struggling bodies. They stumbled against the leg of a brazier, which crashed forward, spilling its glowing coals over the floor. A man who had started to pursue them stepped on the coals, lost his balance, and sprawled in a heap. Other men tripped over him and collapsed in a tangle of flying skirts.

Grateful now for the obscuring clouds of smoke that billowed through the room, Christy reached the door and tugged at the bolt. For one heart-stopping moment, it stuck. Then Mel placed her hand over Christy's and, together, they slammed back the bolt and yanked open the door.

"Run!" Christy yelled.

They ran. Coughing, choking, gasping, they ran. They ran through the shop and out into the street. They ran through gardens, backyards, parking lots, through an endless maze of streets and alleys. They collapsed, panting, behind a hedge, then ran again when distant sirens wailed like bitter ghosts. They ran, fell, hid, rested, ran again.

At last they reached the safety of Christy's home. They dashed into the house, locked the doors, turned on all the lights and huddled together in a corner until time for the early news.

"Around two thirty this morning, fire gutted a local home, which was connected to an antique store," announced the reporter as the camera panned over the smoking ruins. "No lives were lost, but the store and home were completely destroyed. Owner Claudia Popadopalus says she will not rebuild, but will move to a different state."

The camera focused on Claudia's soot-stained face. She glared straight into the camera, straight into Christy's eyes. Christy caught her breath as Claudia's mind brushed hers.

Come, Christina, come, she commanded.

Christy pushed herself erect, holding Claudia's gaze with her own. "You have no power over me," she said aloud.

And knew, with the strength of one who has faced fire and triumphed, that it was true.

Four months later in another town, a girl stopped at a booth in a flea market. She picked up a snake bracelet and wrapped it around her arm. "Hey, I've got to have this!" she cried. "Can I go ahead and wear it?"

The swarthy woman in the booth smiled and nodded her head, causing her coin earrings to jangle. "Of course you must wear it. You have been chosen."

ABOUT MADGE HARRAH

Nancy Drew and I grew up together in the Missouri Ozarks. We moved in different circles, of course. She drove a car, I rode a bicycle. Her father allowed her to travel around the countryside by herself and solve mysteries, my parents expected me home each day for lunch and dinner. On time. Nancy dealt with murderers and thieves, I had to deal with a younger brother who dropped earthworms down the back of my neck. I got even with him, though. On summer nights, while the wind moaned overhead through the catalpa leaves, I told him ghost stories that scared him into nightmares.

Then we moved into a real haunted house. A tall Victorian monstrosity, the house dripped wooden icicles from all the eaves. The ghost stayed quiet while our parents were around, but stalked my brother and me through the rooms when we were alone. We both heard his—or her—stealthy footsteps, we both caught glimpses of a misty purplish shape on the stairs, tinted by the light that streamed through two stained-glass windows, one blue, one bloodred. Nancy was no help. She preferred to tear off in her convertible, leaving my brother and me to face this horror alone.

Such experiences leave their mark. Even now in my dreams I flee down the corridors of that house, pursued by something dreadful that I cannot see. That house comes back in "The Chosen," hiding secrets behind an innocent facade. In college I studied the myths of ancient Crete. Now those gods and goddesses are back. Our daughter once wore a gold bracelet with ruby eyes, a bracelet that gave me the shivers. Now that bracelet is back, too. For that is where I get ideas—from pieces of my life.

Nancy Drew is also back. I sometimes run into her in the local library. She still looks like a teenager and drives that cool sports car while I drive a boring four-door family sedan. Oh, well. I can't stay jealous of her for I owe her a lot. She is the one who first introduced me to mysteries.

Thank you, Nancy. And thank you, Ghost, whoever you are—or were. Rest in peace.

MADGE HARRAH, winner of twelve national and international writing awards, studied with Rod Serling (*The Twilight Zone*). She has since published novels, plays, short stories and articles for adults and also for young readers. Her historical novel, *Honey Girl*, won the National Golden Spur Award for "best juvenile fiction of 1990." Her mystery novel, *No Escape*, and contemporary novel, *The Nobody Club*, won awards in the juvenile fiction category in national contests sponsored by the National League of American Pen Women. In addition, she has won awards for her gothic mysteries for adults, published under the pseudonym Monique Hara.

The neck is broken. I want to reach in and fix it. But I can't because I know as sure as I know anything that if I reach in there that Paul is going to grab me by the wrists and pull me in with him. That's what he wants, is to pull me in with him. It's what he's been waiting for.

BEARING PAUL
BY CHRIS LYNCH

If you've never thought about it, then you've never thought. That's how I took at it, Pauly. And it's not as if this was the first time I ever thought it, either, so this is nothing special, right, and there's no reason to make it out to be anything special. It's happened before, it's happening again, and then it will stop.

Stop it, Paul. I want you to stop it.

Paul lays there in the casket, maybe a foot in front of my face. They thought it would be appropriate to have him wearing his junior varsity baseball jacket over his shirt and tie, to remind us how vital and active and playful he was. Silver satin, with an embroidered red knight on horseback. His hair too is like satin, long and black against the shiny billowing white bath of silk lining that fills the casket like bubbles.

So it's all slick in there, and makes no sound, causes no friction, draws nobody's notice, when Paul wants to shift his shoulders, or turn his head a bit, or quake. Just for me.

I can do what I have to do, Pauly. I can do my part in this. I can carry you out. If only you'll stop it.

The first time was when my old man died. He moved. I know he moved. He moved when I was kneeling there up so close to him while he was being so dead, being so gone, but still—and how was I supposed to figure this, at six years old—but still being so very much my dad.

But that was different. He moved because I *made* him move, by wanting it so bad. And he moved because he owed it to me, the bastard. The least he could do. I was only little. He had no right.

Tipped his head, though, tipped it just oh so little a bit so I could see it, me his boy, and nobody else. Somethin' special, kid, just between you and me. Our little secret. And a version of a wink to go along with it. A reverse wink, where he cracked open the one eye just a slit while the other stayed closed like it was supposed to be when a guy was in a casket surrounded by silk.

It was nice. It was just ours. He owed me that. I liked that he didn't show anybody else, not even my mom. But that was why they had to take it away from me. My fat uncle coming up behind and lifting me by the shoulders because, I don't know, maybe I did stay too long and maybe I did make some sounds, but so what. I had a right. And it wasn't enough any-how, and I would have gotten more, I would have got him sitting all the way up and smiling at me even with sewed lips if they didn't pull me away. Because I wanted it just that bad. And he owed me.

Which was what made that different, Paul. You don't owe me anything, so I wish you'd just stop it.

And like when my Aunt Rita moved her finger. That was different, too, because she had to have that ring on that fin-ger. That ring that belonged to Granma, and was the only thing my mom wanted when she died because Granma promised it would always be Ma's. But Rita had to have it, and when she died she had to take it with her and she was killing my mom at the same time, that stupid ring, Granma's ring, glistening up from that same kind of casket as my dad's only with the purple satin.

She knew, of course, because dead people know. Rita knew

what I was thinking when it was my turn and I was kneeling there and I was wondering when would be the perfect right time. Rita had gotten fat lately, so I was wondering what it was going to take, but I was going to chew the finger off if I had to but she was not taking my mom's ring into the hole with her.

Which of course was when she wiggled the finger. Nothing else had to happen, did it. That was enough, to make my spine trill, my hands go numb on the mini-altar rail. Her hands were folded just like that across her stomach, the ring caught the light above and sparkled right at me as she lifted just that ring finger as if to dare me, sonofabitch boy, just you try and take this ring.

So what I think I know is, you get the movement when something's not right. When something's not right, things can't be finished. Even the dead know that. Especially the dead know that.

But you don't realize until you provoke them, do you? Unless you make them come out of it for you, you don't know that when you come to the wake for the show, when you scoot up close for your look, for your sniff.

You don't know, that you are *their* show.

Tell me Pauly, now that you know. Doesn't everybody think what I'm thinking? Doesn't everybody think they see it move, but we don't tell each other? Isn't this okay that I think this?

I'm a pallbearer for Paul. Which is not right. A fourteen-year-old guy shouldn't be a pallbearer for anybody, and nobody should be a pallbearer for a fourteen-year-old guy. But here we are, the two of us.

Paul was my cousin and we were friends. Not best friends, not closest cousins, but cousin plus friend plus fourteen equals I'm here. Boy pallbearer. The others are all men. I'm here to remind people that Paul was a boy, as if they might have forgotten him already.

Yesterday afternoon was the wake. Last night was the wake. The night before and the afternoon before, too. Four sessions, four times I came up here to be with Paul up close and stayed past my time and nobody broke it up until they had to.

And Paul's been doing things to me. Haven't you, Pauly? See Paul doesn't move when I talk to him. Some kind of a rule, I suppose, that dead folks don't answer when you want them to. So I talk to him a lot now. More and more and more. So he'll stop, and so he'll stay stopped.

This morning is the funeral. It seemed like a long way to this morning. Eight-fifteen service in the funeral home, nine-thirty mass, ten-thirty burial at New Calvary.

Seems like a long way to ten-thirty.

The paper had a little thing about the tragedy. Papers always do that, have a little thing about tragedies involving kids. People must be very interested in that genre. I know I am. There wasn't a teenager who died all last year who didn't wind up seeming like me by the time I was done reading. Paul's tragedy was extra tragic, wasn't it, Pauly? Because it was in that subgenre they call "a senseless tragedy." Young life snuffed out for no good reason. Carelessness. Shouldn't be swimming late at night in that black quarry, now should we. Probably shouldn't be swimming there in the daytime. But we know that. Those of us who swim there, we know that.

Those of us who were there that night, we know that's true.

Those who were there know that's true.

Those there know what's true.

We know, don't we, Pauly. I know, and you know. And you

know what I know about that night. And you're not going to let me forget.

The first afternoon of the wake, Paul fluttered his eyelids. Like someone getting electrical shocks, Paul's eyelashes beat at the air, over and over and over, so long, so much longer than I have ever seen a body twitch before, that I turned around, to see if anybody else could tell.

The line of people stood primly behind me. Just waiting.

When I'd turned back to Paul, he was still again. Don't pull this crap on me, Paul, I don't like it.

"So what if I was saying something? I'm saying good-bye, all right?"

This time it's a funeral home employee moving me along. He seems embarrassed, because what kind of rat shoos a kid away from saying his good-byes to a dead boy. Only I should thank him, Pauly, because I wish someone would or could drag me away from you, or drag you away from me because enough is enough already. The truth is, I *wish* I was saying good-bye to you, but I'm afraid that I'm not. Not yet, anyway, am I right, Paul?

The second time, during the first evening wake hours, seven to nine on Wednesday, Paul pursed his lips. Like when one guy tells a big fat lie and the other guys says, ya, right, kiss me why don't ya.

They have the casket open even in the church, the top half of it's open, anyway, but that's more than enough, I think. He doesn't give me a break, Paul doesn't, not even when I'm only filing past him to get my communion. I'm thinking about it, thinking about how good he looks anyway even despite what happened and even though he's dead now three days. And I look at him, of course, as I pass, and I think, except for the one thing, the neck. Where the neck was broken. Maybe it shifted during the ride over, but you can see it, the way it doesn't lay quite right, where it slightly changes course, turning where a neck isn't supposed to turn. Showing, reminding everybody of exactly how Paul died, which is exactly what is not supposed to show.

I look at it as I pass, and it is striking to me, and perverse, that broken crook of Pauly's neck, and I know where he got it.

And then zing, Pauly pulls it tight and straight again as if somebody'd yanked both ends of the spinal cord like a taut rope.

This time I don't even look around to see if anyone else has witnessed. I know this show is for me alone.

I don't take communion in my palm because my hand is shaking too hard. I take it on my tongue, turn and go back. I try not to, but it's useless now, so I peek again as I pass Paul again and the neck is broken again.

Again. The neck is broken again.

I want to reach in and fix it. I want it not to be broken, and I want to be the one to fix it. But I can't because I know as sure as I know anything that if I reach in there that Paul is going to grab me by the wrists and pull me in with him. That's what he wants, is to pull me in with him. It's what he's been waiting for.

It's okay mostly when I don't have to see him. He leaves me alone mostly when I'm not seeing him. I don't sleep so well at night yet, but that's not Paul's doing exactly, not directly, and I expect that problem to get better.

As soon as I don't have to see him at all. They close the top half of the box now as I stand beside it getting ready for the procession out of the church. That should be it, has to be it. There will be no more viewings of Paul. Paul, there will be no more viewings of you. Wake's done, funeral's done. The box will not be opened again, so you're done, too, Pauly. You're done.

I walk alongside the box to the hearse. I do my small part to lift the box into the back. I ride in the motorcade two black cars back from Paul's body, a nice distance, and we're almost there.

We stop at the site. Everyone gets out. A short walk now, over to the hole, lay him down. And it'll be over, it can be over. I do my small part again, and I think I'm the only one nervous. Paul's uncles aren't nervous, the teacher isn't nervous. My hand slips twice with the sweat, the brass handle sliding right out of my hand. No one even seems to notice as I regrip.

One small problem, the dip in the terrain. A short little hill we have to walk down before we reach the plot. The guys in front, like me, we go down, go down, while the rear guys are up high still.

Bump. Bu-bump. Twice. Inside the box Pauly shifts two times as we're coming down the hill. Like he slid down onto his feet—unless I'm holding his head end—inside the casket. Did he fall on his head again? Did his neck bend, did it break, again? It happened twice in there, and it was hard and loud and unmistakable, like he crashed his head, pushed himself off, then crashed again. Did he break his neck again and again?

Does it hurt, Pauly? Can it hurt, again and again?

I look around me now, and nobody seems to notice a thing. I'm no longer touching the brass handle I'm supposed to be carrying. I let my hand hang there over the handle, but I'm not touching it as we set the casket down at the grave.

He's going in there. Pauly you're going in there. He's in there. Throw your handfuls of dirt, people, because I'm going now. And when I'm gone whoever does it is going to come and cover that hole with a half-ton of dirt and it's going to stay there and you're going to stay there, too, Paul.

Good-bye, Pauly. I'm sorry. I told you that already, and I don't have to tell you that anymore. But I am. Sorry.

Good-bye is good-bye, Pauly.

And whoever it is is going to have that hole packed tight before I try to sleep tonight. The earth covers you, the night covers me, and good-bye is good-bye, Pauly.

It's ten o'clock and I go to bed but I don't sleep. It was supposed to be done by now, but it doesn't feel like it's done.

It's eleven o'clock and I'm still in bed but I still don't sleep.

It's twelve o'clock and maybe I slept for a few minutes but not now.

It's two A.M. and I'm not sleeping for good, because Paul is here, which isn't supposed to be.

"Good-bye is good-bye, Paul," I say, moving nothing but my eyes.

"Get up," he says.

"Good-bye is good-bye, Paul. It's done now."

"Good-bye is good-bye, but it ain't done yet. Get up."

"No, Pauly, I won't get up. I won't move from here. You have to be gone now."

"I ain't never going to be gone if you don't get up."

I get up. Because whatever it is he's going to do to me, it cannot be worse than his never going away.

"Put your suit on," he says. "But you won't need a towel."

The cliff above the quarry is about seventy feet high. I don't feel cold, standing there, even though the wind is pushing at me steadily. There is room on this ledge for the two of us and a few empty beer bottles, but not much else. Below, the water looks calm and still, looks deep, even, in its blackness. A sharp granite boulder pokes its crest out of the water here and there, so that you might think you know where the bad spots are. You might.

Paul is standing with his toes hanging over the edge of the cliff, his back to me.

"What am I doing?" I ask.

"You know what you're doing," he says.

"No, Pauly, I don't."

"You're finishing," he says.

"What finishing? I'm not not finished with anything."

"I ain't the school guidance counselor. I know you ain't done."

"Well I say I'm done."

Paul does not turn to me. He stares and stares straight down at the quarry that he knows now better than anyone knows it.

"Remember you said it yourself. The movement. You get it when things aren't right. And things aren't right, are they?"

"No," I say almost down in a whisper. "They're not."

For a moment, there is a relief there. That I can say it finally.

"And the movement ain't going to stop, as long as it ain't right. No matter how many tons of dirt they put on me."

Then, Paul turns to me. Just his head, turning way, way around while his shoulders remain squared the other way. "I was trying to tell you before. Didn't you hear me knocking for you today?"

He smiles at me in a way that makes me want to jump, to fly past him and away. Then he looks back toward the water.

"So now all you have to do is finish. Jump, like you were supposed to when I jumped. Which you forgot to do."

"I'm not jumping."

"Okay. Let's go home, then."

There is a long silence as Paul stands on the edge looking down, and I stand looking at his back.

"No, Pauly, you can't go home with me. I can't take any more of that."

"Finish it, then. You'll probably come through it fine. Me, I just made a mistake. You won't do that, because you're smart. You were always smarter than me, weren't you? You always did the smarter thing."

He still doesn't look at me. He is right there in front of me, so close that if I reach out I can place my hand flat on his back.

"So if I jump, it's done?"

"So if you do, it is."

He knows I can't do it. If I could, I would have done it the first time. He also knows I can't bear one more day of what he's doing to me. Every way I turn, I find me a coward.

Without a second of reflection, I explode on him, driving with my legs, reaching out with both hands to shove Paul off the cliff.

And I'm airborne. Out eight, ten feet from the face of the cliff, I'm falling, my hands are out in front of me, my ears pounding with the whistling wind. I stare at the biggest jagged granite chunk, growing before my eyes, and I blow out my lungs in a scream that makes no sound.

They know, the dead folks do. Pauly said that would end it, and it ended it. I lie in bed, staring up at the ceiling, my hands folded gently across my chest, and I am rested for the first time in a week. Paul doesn't come and see me anymore, even though whole crowds of other people file by.

Good-bye is good-bye, Pauly.

About Chris Lynch

I wrote "Bearing Paul" because I felt, as a child, and still feel today, as if every dead body I've seen appeared to move just a little bit. And I think many other people see it as well, but it remains a shadowy secret because we never compare notes. I've decided here to show my notes.

The story is also about guilt. Guilt brought on by our acts. Guilt brought on by our failures to act. And guilt that comes out of no place but feels just as bad. It's about what we can do to ourselves if we let guilt take us over. It's about the phantasms we can create.

Chris Lynch lives in Boston with his wife, Tina Coviello, and their two children, Sophia and Walker. A graduate of Boston's Suffolk University with a degree in journalism, Mr. Lynch also holds a Master of Arts degree from the writing program at Emerson College in Boston, where he later taught creative writing. In the period between graduating Suffolk and attending Emerson, he worked as a proofreader of financial reports, a house painter, and as a truck driver moving furniture. Presently, Mr. Lynch is a stay-at-home father who, in addition to working with young beginning writers on a one-on-one basis, continues to write.

CHRIS LYNCH is the author of *Shadow Boxer, Iceman,* and *Gypsy Davey* (all ALA Best Books for Young Adults and ALA Recommended Books for the Reluctant Young Adult Reader.) His most recent novels are *Slot Machine* and the "Blue-Eyed Son" trilogy.